I0684606

Diamonds N' Roses

Vogue

Crown Jewelz Publishing

Diamonds N' Roses
Part V of The Diamond Collection
Copyright ©2016 Vogue

ISBN-13: 978-0-9888004-5-8
ISBN-10: 0-9888004-5-4

All rights reserved. Printed in the United States of America.
No part of this book may be used or reproduced in any manner whatsoever
without written permission except in the case of brief quotations embodied
in articles and reviews.

Cover Design by Vogue

Website: www.simplyvogue.net

This book is a work of fiction. References to real people, events,
establishments, organizations, or locales are intended only to provide a sense
of authenticity, and are used fictitiously. All other characters and all incidents
and dialogue are drawn from the author's imagination and are not to be
construed as "real."

The Wedding

THE BRIDE
Carmen Denise Davenport

THE GROOM
Jay Santiago

THE MATRON OF HONOR
Tiara Washington

THE BEST MAN
Malik Washington

THE MAID OF HONOR
Kristian Olivia Kane

THE BRIDESMAID
Akaila DeGonzaza - Kane

THE GROOMSMEN
Malachi DeGonzaza- Kane
Guillermo "Gully" Perez- Santiago

THE FLOWER GIRL
Nyla Jaslene Santiago

THE RING BEARER
Rakim Antonio Santiago

THE OFFICIANT
Silvas Achilles

Love suffers long and is kind; love does not envy; love does not parade itself, is not puffed up; does not behave rudely, does not seek its own, is not provoked, thinks no evil; does not rejoice in iniquity, but rejoices in the truth; bears all things, believes all things, hopes all things, endures all things. Love never fails. But whether there are prophecies, they will fail; whether there are tongues, they will cease; whether there is knowledge, it will vanish away.

1 Corinthians 13: 4-8 NKJV

1

The Lion's Den
December

Barely eleven o'clock, Sapphire was already in full swing and nearing capacity. Located in the heart of downtown East Brookstone, the dance club served as the official after party for the reopening of Blue Magic, one of the city's popular eateries. Wall to wall with the who's who of New York, the venue was a media paradise. The VIP lounges were overflowing with ballers and rappers as well as their respective entourages. Somewhat uncomfortable with the over crowdedness, Carmen made her way inside of Jay's second floor office to escape the mayhem.

The office was dim since the house lights were off to prevent any interference with the lighting experience below. Currently lit a sapphire blue, the lighting had been paired with strobe lights and other dramatic effects. The mood was overly cinematic, which Carmen noticed as she watched the scene from a large glass window. Her eyes danced continuously around the club until she spotted her fiancé walking through the crowd. Never alone, Jay was flanked by his right-hands, Roman and Gully, as they conducted their nightly walkthrough.

Their first stop was the main DJ booth which was lined with exotic-looking women. Two of the club's employees were in the mix as well. Nicholas and Phase were two former members of the Santiago cartel who now handled various tasks within the club. Jay approached them first, and since their conversation was inaudible, Carmen focused her attention elsewhere. A movie theater-sized video screen was mounted to the left wall of the club and standing in front of it was none other than her and Jay's eldest son, King. His girlfriend, Coco, was with him, along with Malik and Tiara, lifelong friends of Carmen and Jay.

"Eight more people and we're out of compliance."

Carmen looked over her shoulder to see Jay standing in the doorway. *Damn, he moves fast*, she thought. "You say that like you don't have that problem every night." She eased out a smile as he locked the office door behind him.

"I told security to keep 'em coming," Jay replied, now heading towards the mini bar. "I don't want the fire marshal on my ass, but a nice little check will keep him quiet." Jay pulled two glasses from the bar's wooden cabinet followed by a bottle of cognac. Although they had been drinking heavily for most of the night, the chances of them slowing down were slim to none. He mixed the cognac with a couple ounces of lemon-lime soda before handing a glass to Carmen. To his surprise, she downed it quickly before asking for more. "You keep drinking like that, I'm gonna have to carry you out of here."

He didn't wait for a response as he made her another drink. He handed it to her, which she took. "Were Kristian and Akaila downstairs?" she asked.

Jay chuckled at the question. Carmen expected her daughters to be on the dance floor, but instead, they were in VIP giving their father's new girlfriend, Monifah, the third degree. It was a fairly new relationship for Carmen's soon-to-be ex-husband, Kane. Obviously, Kristian and Akaila weren't pleased with his selection. "They're downstairs being teenage girls," he joked. Her daughters were ripping Monifah to shreds, a humorous feat, which didn't need interruption. Therefore, he changed the subject. "Time was up a while ago."

Carmen grabbed a bottle of VSOP from the counter and poured herself another drink. His words referenced her miscarriage, a tragic event, which occurred only four short months ago. Their plan was to try again yet there had been little intimacy. He hadn't pressured her, but it was obvious, he was long overdue. If he asked, Carmen would admit she was, too.

"You're getting quiet on me."

Carmen knew she appeared to be at a loss for words. Truly not the case. She parted her lips to speak until he snatched her glass out her hand. He set it at the far end of the mini bar as if she was using it as a distraction. Taking the hint, she wiped her palms on her lace dress. Once dry, her fingers found their way to his bowtie. Jay followed suit, removing his black tuxedo jacket as if he sensed her plan.

"Most stylists don't undress their clients," he whispered once her hands started unbuttoning his shirt. "I guess you can add this to my tab."

His words made a small smile appear on Carmen's face as she started to unhook the bars on his trousers. Simultaneously, he pulled off his shirt, his chiseled arms on full display. Not once had she seen him workout yet he maintained a physique as perfect as his hazel eyes. Half dressed in front of her, Carmen carefully examined him until his touch became a distraction. His hands had been circling her waist, but now she felt his fingertips trickling down her spine. Then, he traveled farther.

Instantly, the temperature rose above the normal seventy degrees as his hands cupped her derriere. With his pants at his ankles, his growing erection could easily be felt due to the thinness of her dress. The imprint made a soft moan escape her lips. She hadn't been touched in months and the idea of being penetrated excited her to the point she quickly removed her heels.

Perfect timing, Jay thought. He made no hesitation to lead her towards the leather loveseat. His pants were still at his ankles as he mounted her on top of him. Naturally, her legs slid apart, which he used to his advantage. One hand raised her dress to her waist while the other moved her panties to the side. Within seconds, his index and middle fingers disappeared deep in her kitty kat, an area he knew well. He massaged her in a circular motion until the sound of her breathing told him she wanted more. His free hand then moved to her zipper. When her dress fell at her knees, Carmen reached behind her and unhooked her bra.

The desire to reach the place where they connected best was stronger than numbers could allow. Carmen was well lubricated due to the work of his fingers, and Jay yearned to feel her inner walls. For months he controlled his urges, but tonight, he was weak. The mere scent of her made him succumb. A satisfying, sweet savor, his tongue slithered around the skin in between her breasts until his lips became fixed on her left nipple. He sucked hard as she glided over his thickness until he felt her tap his chest. He took the hint, loosening his grip, allowing his tongue to circle around her areola. Carmen then heightened their lovemaking, closing her legs around his manhood. A move she did so her love box could feel tighter; it transported him out of reality. The feel-good friction sent him to an outer space of euphoria only for him to crash into a state of orgasmic bliss.

Meanwhile, down below them, the after party remained in effect. Bottles were popped left and right, the club now over its legal capacity. Kane stood in a central area of the club although he was ready to go hours ago. Earlier that evening, he showed up to the reopening of Blue Magic to discover his girlfriend had been lying about her identity. He met her as Jean Monet only to learn she was born Monifah Harris and was a distant friend of his soon-to-be ex-wife, Carmen. Still salty over the matter, he watched the party in a sulk until he couldn't bare the atmosphere.

To his dismay, he and Monifah had ridden together. He had to check in with her before he left so she would know he was headed home. He remembered seeing her last in VIP, which was where he headed until his pace was slowed by the crowd. He looked for a way of escape amidst the throngs of people and in the process, saw something move near the ceiling. He assumed it was a shadow from a light fixture until the image became more focused. He then recognized it to be his wife. He watched her in agony as her nude body moved snake-like over Jay's.

It was the second time he caught them in the act except this time it was public. Due to the large crowd, Kane knew he wasn't the only one watching. Voyeurs were getting a free show with the exception of a cover charge. For Kane, the ordeal was more disturbing than pleasurable. Now filled with a growing rage, he pushed his way through the crowd in an attempt to get to the office. Obscenities were thrown in his direction, which he ignored. However, when he looked at the office window again and saw Carmen's mouth make an O, he stopped.

For years he had seen his wife make the same expression. A look that stroked his ego, it told him he'd satisfied her every need. Based off what he was seeing, Jay had done the same. The idea of them being intimate sent Kane into a spell of temporary insanity. He blocked out the people around him, the music, and even the strobe lights. The world around him became a blur until a piercing scream interrupted his trance. The sound startled him, but it was too late. He had already pulled the trigger.

2

All Things Go

Carmen sat straight up, sweat dripping steadily from her brow. The sound of gunshots was repetitive in her ear until she realized it was her alarm clock. Now wide awake, she quickly turned it off, silencing the noise. What she thought was a typical wet dream ended up being nothing short of a night terror. She had gone from reliving her rendezvous with Jay to having Kane shoot them dead. It was her first time having sex in public, a result of hitting the bottle too hard, and the nightmare made her want to stick to the bedroom.

Coming to grips that the vision wasn't completely reality, she laid down in bed. Jay hadn't stirred so she used the time to talk to God. By the time she was finished with her prayer, Jay's alarm was going off, which meant it was seven o'clock. He moved beside her yet he didn't bother to turn it off. Somewhat annoyed by it, Carmen got up and pressed the snooze button. She was unsure of his schedule for the day, so she took advantage of the time and headed to the shower. Jay didn't wake until she was completely dressed and even then, he remained in bed.

"You should work a half day."

Carmen chuckled at the comment. She had already taken an extended leave and the last thing she needed was more time off. Her absence had strongly impacted her business and she was just now able to start preparing for the launch of her new clothing line, *Fresh Prince*. "It would be nice, but it's not possible. I have two big meetings today. One of 'em is with our wedding planners. Remember?"

"I didn't forget, I plan on—" Jay was interrupted by the sound of his phone. He automatically assumed his cousin, Gully, was calling him, since he was his driver for the day. However, the number showing on the screen wasn't programmed in his phone. It had a 212 area code, which meant the number was local. Despite his conversation with Carmen, he answered the call. Very little noise was on the line, which he took notice of. "Hello."

"Howard Grendel for Jay Santiago," the person greeted.

Jay sat up straight, realizing who was on the other end. Howard Grendel was the man responsible for bringing the surveillance footage of the shooting at Blue Magic to the attention of several prominent New York judges. The footage got him a bail variation, which resulted in his immediate release from jail. Currently awaiting trial, he remembered his lawyer, Gomez, telling him Grendel was a part of Amnesty International. "Speaking," Jay replied. "Let me first tell you thank you."

"No thanks needed, Mr. Santiago. I'm sorry to bother you so early, but I need to meet with you. I got your number through your lawyer, Gomez. Let's say I need a favor for a favor. Can we meet for breakfast?"

"That's fine. Blue Magic is usually my first stop. We can meet there. Is nine okay? There's a conference room available on the third floor if privacy is an issue."

"That sounds good, Mr. Santiago. I will see you then."

Jay parted his lips to say goodbye, but Grendel had already hung up. Unsure of what favor he needed, he pulled the phone from his ear, immediately going to his Google app. He knew very little about Amnesty International, but he could always learn. Quickly typing in the words, he stopped when Carmen's shadow came over him.

"I meet with the planners at nine," she announced, continuing their conversation. "Did you suddenly forget? What was said on that call that made you forget about our wedding?"

Jay set his phone in his lap now aware of his error. He assumed the meeting with Grendel wouldn't take long; however, he didn't know what he wanted. It could be something minor or something which acquired more attention than a planning session for a wedding that was more than a year away. "It's something quick. I'll only be a few minutes late," he responded. "If I can't make it, I know you can handle it. I trust you. I'll make the next one."

Carmen narrowed her eyes. She was certain Jay was going to say yes prior to his phone call. Something else was obviously more important than their upcoming nuptials. She would admit there was plenty of time to prepare, but it was an occasion that required work on both their parts. She wanted him to be as hands-on as she was. Unfortunately, her wants weren't a factor that morning. Somewhat accepting of his potential absence, she told him okay before leaving the room to check on Rakim and Nyla.

Their youngest two, both toddlers, were in their rooms fast asleep. She spent a few minutes with each one, watching as they slumbered, until it was time to head to Flame. Her company was an inheritance from her mother which she turned into a multi-million dollar fashion empire. She walked in her building promptly at eight-thirty and on to the executive floor. The elevator doors hadn't even closed behind her before her receptionist, Cathy, was in her face, completely out of breath.

"Coco Masterson is here," Cathy announced. "She's anxious to talk to you."

Carmen peered around the corner to see Coco standing in front of Cathy's desk. Not quite sure why she was there, she gave Cathy a look of inquisition. Her receptionist shrugged her shoulders, obviously clueless about the visit. While it wasn't awkward, it was unexpected. Thankfully, she had a window of time to kill before her wedding planners showed up.

"Good morning," she greeted, now approaching Coco. "You threw me for a loop. Did your mother send you here to try and get exclusive rights to my wedding?" Coco was the daughter of the editor-in-chief of *XXL* magazine so Carmen expected the joke to garner a response. Coco, however, didn't smile or flinch. She simply stood there clutching her purse as if it contained a million dollars. "I guess not. So, what's going on?"

"Can we?" Coco asked, pointing at Carmen's office.

"Of course," Carmen replied. She led the way inside and once Coco came in, she closed the door behind them. Coco didn't bother to sit so she remained standing as well. "What is it? You're scaring me." She tried to force a smile, which turned upside down when she saw Coco digging in her purse. When she pulled out a Ziploc bag, Carmen sat down. She covered her mouth to keep from screaming because her son's 18-year-old girlfriend was holding a pregnancy test. To make matters worse, she was handing it to her.

"I was in denial, but I'm not anymore."

Carmen didn't take the pregnancy test from her. She was no longer covering her mouth, this time covering her eyes. There she was, still in her early forties, wanting to have more kids while her eldest son, King, was making her a grandmother. Too much for her to handle, Carmen stood up and paced the floor. *This can't be happening. King can't be having sex. I mean, Coco can't be having sex. When did they do it? Was his little brother home? What if they had sex and Malachi heard? Shit, forget about Malachi, what about Jay? He is going to blow the roof.*

"You're the first one I've told. I called Kristian, but she didn't pick up." Coco looked at the test in her hands and then at Carmen. "My mother is going to kill me," she cried, changing the subject. "How did this happen? I'm supposed to be transferring to Brookstone University in the spring. If I'm four months pregnant, I'll be having this baby in either May or June. I'll be further behind."

Carmen took a deep breath as she tried to think on her toes. "Have you told your parents? Have you said anything to King? Shit, wait, you just said I'm the first one you told." Carmen paused so she could gather her thoughts. She took a few moments to calm herself before she spoke. "I know you're scared. Believe me, I do. I've been there. I wasn't as young as you, but I was there. You're not alone, though. King is well equipped to make sure you and the baby have everything you need. You might have to take a break from school, but you can always go back." Carmen exhaled because she knew school and money wasn't the issue. It was her son's maturity. She didn't know if he was ready to be a father especially when he was still dealing with his own daddy issues.

Coco shook her head repeatedly. "My mother will kill me before I even give birth. I came here because I need money for an abortion. I can borrow it from you. Once I'm better, I can book a modeling gig and pay you back."

Carmen grabbed her desk for support at Coco's plans. Not once did the idea of abortion cross her mind. While it wasn't her place to convince her to do otherwise or push her religious beliefs, she definitely couldn't give her the money. "Coco, I know telling your mother is a scary thing. But, do you really think she would want you to have an abortion? How would it make her feel to know you made this decision without consulting her? You haven't even talked to King."

"You know my mother, Ms. Davenport. She hates King. If she knew I lost my virginity to him, she would kill us both. Once she finds out I'm pregnant, she's gonna bury us alive."

Carmen's feet shifted at how overly dramatic Coco was being. Maya wasn't King's biggest fan, but she had learned to accept him over the years. "What we can do, Coco, is this. Tonight, I'll have a dinner at my house, let's say seven o'clock. Invite your parents, bring King. We'll discuss this like adults."

"Ms. Davenport, can I just have the money? I can make the appointment. I don't want to be a mother. I don't want to be pregnant. Please, I'll pay you back."

Carmen mouthed the word no before saying it out loud. "I can't give you the money. What I can give you is love, support, and prayer. Now, I can meet with King on my lunch break. Do you want to come? I'll hold your hand while you tell him the news."

Coco's tears were flowing more heavily because she'd hit a brick wall. King's mother was her only resort. "Please," she begged, gripping the Ziploc bag. "I'm not ready for this. I need to finish school."

"You can finish school. Look at what I built, fresh out of prison with a baby." Carmen extended her arms to illustrate. "I had felonies, no degree, and a child." Carmen dropped her arms at her side as Coco wept. She looked pitiful, which made her latch onto her. "I know you're scared. I was scared, too, but you have so many people around you who love you. We'll be there through all of this. You can still finish school and model. I promise you."

Coco heard her clearly yet she wasn't completely set on keeping the baby. She would admit she was being slightly selfish, making the decision before even talking to King. She didn't even know how she was going to break the news to him. Perhaps it wasn't a question of how, but rather of when. As if it was to be that moment, she listened as Carmen's cell phone rung.

"Stay right here," Carmen ordered as she broke the embrace. "Don't go anywhere." She reached for her phone to see *Kane* flashing on the screen. Automatically, her mind went to the nightmare she had. She shivered at the thought before answering the call. "Mr. Kane," she greeted. "How can I help you?"

"Kristian is gone."

"Don't say that to me. What do you mean she's gone?"

"Well, some of her things are missing. I think she did it. I think she went to Georgia to see Victor. You know he made bail this weekend."

Carmen closed her eyes and swallowed at the same time. So much was going on; she was trying her best to keep it straight in her head. *And to think*, Carmen thought, *I thought my only concern for today would be my freakin' wedding. Now I'm dealing with a pregnancy and a missing child—again.*

It was only four months ago when her eldest daughter was kidnapped by Blu, a disgruntled drug kingpin. The kidnapping was a part of his retaliation for being kicked out of Jay's cartel. Kristian claimed Blu's business partner, Victor, was her knight in shining armor throughout the whole ordeal. She repeatedly begged to go to Georgia to check on him after Blu put him flat on his back in an Atlanta hospital. After he was well enough to be discharged, he was taken to jail after being charged with Kristian's kidnapping. Now free, Carmen assumed her daughter had made her way down South. Majorly annoyed by the news, Carmen's true feelings came out in her tone.

"Get on a plane and find her. Don't call me until you have your hands around her neck."

"I can't," Kane replied. "My money is low. I can't afford a plane ticket. That's what I need to talk to you about. I need to borrow some money. I can't get it from Monifah because we're not together anymore. I broke up with her right after we left Sapphire Saturday night. You know I don't have a job. My savings is down to nothing."

Well, well, well, Carmen thought. *I knew the day was going to come. If he thinks I'm going to be his ATM, he's got another thing coming. He's going to have to work for every penny I give him.* "Go ahead and pay for the ticket. If you can squeeze in fifteen minutes, submit an application on our Career portal. I'll give you a job working security. It runs about seventy grand a year. I'll even formally approve it so you can skip the interview. Just make sure you get up here to complete your paperwork before you leave. There's money in petty cash so make sure you call Cathy to get it. Just don't be foolish with it."

"Thank you. I know that—"

Carmen hung up the phone before he could finish. She didn't have time to listen to Kane rattle. At this point, Kristian could be hemmed up in Timbuktu.

"What's wrong?" Coco asked.

"Nothing we can't handle," Carmen replied. She flashed a smile to ease her worries. "Look, I have a meeting in a few minutes. I'm going to text King about lunch. Make sure you tell your parents about dinner, okay?"

Coco nodded her head despite her uneasiness. She wanted to live past the age of eighteen, but the chances would be slim once her mother learned of her pregnancy. She wasn't even sure how King was going to react and planned on dodging all his calls. If she was lucky, she would spend the majority of the day vomiting so she wouldn't have to talk to anyone. She was certain all hell was about to break loose and went home to prepare for it.

***

Unlike Coco, Jay's meeting with Howard Grendel was impromptu, but he was well prepared. For the past thirty minutes he had been familiarizing himself with Amnesty International. The group, founded in London, England, was largely known for its focus on human rights and funded solely by donations and member fees. In the event Grendel was seeking money, he was well prepared to donate no less than a hundred thousand to the cause.

Checkbook in hand, he walked towards the third floor conference room of Blue Magic to see Grendel already seated. A glass of orange juice was at each place setting along with a plate of food, but Grendel had touched neither. Well aware he was waiting on him, Jay made his presence known. "Good morning," he welcomed. Jay pulled out his chair, sitting down in front of the brown-haired man. "I'm glad I'm able to finally put a face to a name."

Grendel responded first with a smile. "I can't say the same. Cameras love you around here, Mr. Santiago." A chuckle sounded out his mouth before he continued. "I did look forward to our conversation. Not everyone is able to get in your inner circle."

"You did me a favor, Grendel. I owe you."

Grendel chuckled again before picking up his glass of orange juice. "You're not indebted to me, Jay. I'm nothing but a messenger. I'm not sure how much you know about Amnesty, but I must first tell you that we don't work with the U.S. government. We pride ourselves on that. From what I've learned of you, you have some sort of secret employment with Uncle Sam."

"An agreement is in place," Jay admitted.

Grendel set his glass down. "What is the agreement? I have a strong feeling you're working for a cause you know nothing about. However, the cause is one I'm very passionate about."

"You know a lot to be someone without any ties to the government," Jay stated. "Then again, you were able to get into Judge McCallum's office to steal my surveillance tape. You have some pull somewhere."

"My uncle works in the White House. When my name became attached to yours, he reached out. Like I need a favor from you, he needed a favor from me." Another small chuckle sounded out Grendel's mouth. "As far as me getting your tape, I was at the courthouse sitting in on another case. It went to recess and while I was in the hallway, I overheard the judge's receptionist telling a lady that a detective was in the judge's chambers. She said he was viewing a surveillance tape from your restaurant. A few minutes later, Detective Kane ran in the hallway screaming. It sounded peculiar to me that the oldest judge in this state would die while viewing your tape. Then, your fiancée's husband was in there with him. That sounded a little fishy. I decided to do some snooping. While Kane was giving statements, I went in the office, found the tape, and took it.

"Enough about me, though," Grendel continued. "Tell me, Mr. Santiago, what did the government ask you to do? I mean, your rap sheet is horrific. They wanted something awfully bad to give you an early release." Grendel waited for Jay to respond and when he didn't, he pressed him further. "Mr. Santiago, it's a simple question. I'm here to ask for a favor, one, which you can say no to. I'm also not out to trick you, unlike *your* government."

Jay didn't appreciate being told he was a pawn. Even if he was, he wouldn't tell Grendel the details of his agreement. "Why don't *you* tell me? You seem to know so much. Educate me on what they have me doing."

Grendel picked up one of the Belgian waffles on his plate. A small pitcher of maple syrup was to the right of him, but he didn't touch it. Instead, he bit into the waffle, chewing quickly before speaking again. "You can be quite difficult, Mr. Santiago. You have a tight lip. That's a good thing. Maybe, I should give away the goods." He took another bite before setting the waffle on his plate. "The U.S. government wants the Pink Sunrise. Or, so they say. It's your job to turn it in. That was the agreement, right? You get in good with Carmen, steal the diamond, and turn it in. Then, they would let you out of a life sentence after serving seventeen years."

Jay's feet shuffled underneath the table. Grendel had hit the nail on the head. Whoever his connect was at the White House had vast knowledge of the deal. The downfall of it all was that the diamond, constructed by Gabi Tolkowsky, was a jewel, which belonged to him. He had the jewel stolen from its rightful owner nearly twenty-something years ago by one of his men, Enosis. It fell into Carmen's hands when she traveled to the Bahamas and murdered Enosis in cold blood to get it. A stone he desperately wanted back due to his own personal interest, he accepted the deal so he could regain his freedom and his jewel. Unfortunately, he hadn't pried the diamond out Carmen's hands, thus not completing his assignment.

"I am correct, aren't I?" Grendel asked.

"Very much so," Jay replied. He grabbed his glass of orange juice, taking a sip. "I stopped trying to find it a long time ago. Matter of fact, my fiancée and I don't even discuss it."

"The U.S. government doesn't care about the Pink Sunrise, Mr. Santiago. What they care about is your connection to diamond mines. We all know it's against the law to import rough diamonds into the United States from certain countries in Africa. Somehow, you're able to do it. I mean, you are opening up a jewelry store."

"I don't import rough diamonds, Mr. Grendel."

"You may not be, but the U.S. government believes you are. They also believe you're purchasing diamonds from someone who is using your money to fund their war efforts. They couldn't care less about you; they want him. Your name attracted their attention because it was your girlfriend who was charged with stealing the sixth largest pink diamond in the world. We both know she wasn't the original thief. That assumption led the government to you. You became a toy in their eyes. Something they could use and manipulate to get what they really wanted. You were released from prison because they knew you were going to find your way to your passion—diamonds. And Mr. Santiago, you did. They want to track you so you can help lead them to the person who is responsible for all this conflict in Africa."

Jay laughed at Grendel's words only because he spoke as if he was in the middle of some brewing war. While he never looked into his business partner's affairs, Jay knew of him to be a wealthy, biracial man with access to various diamond mines in Sierra Leone and Liberia. He met him through mutual friends and their relationship was more business than personal. "I'm sorry," Jay told him, chuckling. "I just don't know who made this stuff up."

Grendel's face was now completely straight. "I know this seems like a joke to you, but it isn't to me. Innocent people are enslaved to pick the diamonds you love. Children are stripped of their youth to fight for reasons they don't even understand. You, like other rich people of the world, have a blind eye to it. My organization works to make issues such as this known. We are a global organization committed to change, which we will do with or without your help."

Jay watched as Grendel stood from his seat. He did the same, asking him repeatedly to stay. Grendel flat out refused, telling him he wasted his time. Jay tried to explain his behavior, but Grendel's mind was made up.

"It would be to your benefit to pick up a newspaper. Educate yourself on blood diamonds. Find out as much as you can about your supplier. That's the best advice I can give you. Once you do, we can have another conversation."

Grendel headed towards the stairwell, leaving Jay with two plates of nearly uneaten food. He had walked in the room with the expectation of writing a check only to receive a lesson on current events. He also didn't expect to learn his release from prison was only a ploy to get close to his partner in Africa. Thankfully, Grendel didn't know his partner's identity so tracks were being covered well. He didn't know how close the government was and wouldn't know unless Grendel agreed to meet with him again. Until then, Jay needed to do his homework.

As he headed out the conference room, he felt his phone vibrate in his pocket. While he hoped it was Grendel, it ended up being Malik. His right-hand had been downstairs during his meeting so he assumed he was ready to head to Sapphire. "I'm about to come down," he told him, walking in the hallway.

"Stay there. Gully and I are on our way up. King's deal went through. Mastermind is going to distribute King Records."

Jay wasn't the least bit surprised at the news. King had been working hard for the past several months trying to get his record label off the ground. Like all Santiagos, he struck gold with whatever he touched. "I wish he was the one telling me this."

"He told me because he wants me to be VP. He even wants Nicholas to be a part of it."

Jay was caught off guard at King's latest scheme. His son was well aware of the various roles Malik played in his businesses. When it came to Nicholas, he covered King's position at Sapphire after he quit. By offering them employment, not only was King forcing Malik and Nicholas to choose between them, he was putting more strain on their relationship. "He—" Jay was silenced at the sound of footsteps on the stairwell. When Malik and Gully came in view, he hung up the phone. "You told him no, didn't you?" Malik wasn't quick to respond, which meant he hadn't. "So you're actually considering this?"

Gully barged in on the conversation to bring up a topic he felt was more important than King's newest business venture. "Do you want me to swing you by Flame? Carmen is meeting with the wedding planners."

"I know about it. I'm asking him about this position, though."

Jay focused his attention on Malik as he waited for a response. "Are you considering this?" Malik gave him a simple shrug of his shoulders. Either his mind wasn't made up or he was too nervous to admit he was accepting a position at King Records. Whichever it was, Jay wasn't going to stand there trying to figure it out. "I don't have time for this. Do what you want." The words rolled off his tongue, although in actuality, he did care about Malik's decision. He only was in a rush to get to King to learn the reason behind his.

3

Want Some More

King sent his mother the news of King Records via text, but the message initially went unread. After Coco's unexpected visit at Flame, Carmen was bombarded by her creative team regarding the promotional campaign for *Fresh Prince*. They didn't make their exit until a few minutes before her wedding planners were scheduled to arrive, which gave her a chance to check her phone. It was then she learned of King's new business venture. He also had accepted her lunch invitation. About to call him, she settled for a quick text of congratulations once Cathy announced her wedding planners had arrived.

Veronica Freeman and Patience Nelson were the brains of Uptown NYC, one of the city's most elite event planning and production companies. The duo had done much more than plan weddings under their DreamGirlz brand. From helping with Broadway plays to assisting with fashion shows, the two were the best of the best.

"Date, time, place, and budget," Veronica stated after they had spent thirty minutes catching up. The wife of the New York Giants' quarterback, she was the business persona of the duo while Patience had the more creative side.

"December 25th of next year, preferably in the afternoon, maybe like three or four p.m.," Carmen responded. "We know it's Christmas Day so we want there to be some time for the kids to open their presents." She picked up a list of ideas she and Jay had jotted down so she could remember to make mention of certain things. "We're getting married in San Juan at Jay's estate so we don't have to worry about a venue. There's a great view of the ocean from his backyard so we want to have the ceremony there."

"And the budget?" Veronica pressed. "How big are we going? Oh, and what colors have y'all talked about?"

Carmen smiled because she knew how the women were going to react when she said the figure. The budget was high compared to most weddings, but it had to be considering the location. "Jay and I agreed on a budget of two million. It gives y'all a lot of wiggle room, but let me explain. With that money, not only do we have to honor the contract, but it also has to cover flights to and from San Juan. We also will need extra security, food, transportation, etc. As far as colors, we're thinking saffron, which is like a golden yellow, jade green, and dove."

"Since you used the word we," Veronica reiterated, "How involved is Jay going to be? I noticed he isn't here."

Carmen let out a large sigh as Veronica reminded her of the last conversation she shared with him. "His attendance was sort of in the air. I guess he couldn't make it." Carmen noticed a quick exchange of glances between Veronica and Patience. Something told her they didn't believe Jay would be involved. While his absence made things look sketchy, Carmen didn't want to doubt his involvement.

"The reason I asked," Veronica began, "is because we're aware of everything going on with him. A lot of work is gonna be put into this wedding. I would hate to see you waste money because things don't work in his favor."

Carmen's eyes naturally blinked at how Veronica tried to butter up her words. She stated she didn't want her to waste her money, but what she really meant was that she didn't want to waste her time. In a way, Carmen wanted to give a slick comment back, but instead she practiced her professionalism. "We're all taking risks here," she began. "Me personally, I like to stay on the positive side of things. Jay has a great defense team and his court date has been set. He's going to be cleared, which is why we're moving forward with the wedding."

The two women exchanged another set of glances, but neither of them commented on what she said. If anything, they went back to discussing details of the wedding as if Jay's criminal charges hadn't been mentioned. Forty-five minutes later, they were leaving her office and she was on the phone with Linx, her driver for the day.

"Schedules got switched," he told her after she asked where he was. "I got Jay right now. Gully is going to scoop you. He should be parked out front."

Sure enough, like Linx said, Carmen walked outside to find Gully in front of Flame. She greeted him once she was inside the limo and gave him her lunch plans. "King and I are eating at Cipriani's. It'll be my treat if you're hungry."

"I'm gonna pass on this one. I actually had an early lunch with Jay and Malik." Gully met eyes with Carmen in the rearview mirror as he pulled away from her building. "I bet your lunch will be better than what I endured. Jay and Malik went at it over this deal for King Records. You know King wants Malik and Nicholas to work for him."

Carmen rolled her eyes as Gully made her aware of another problem in her household. Not only was her wedding planning starting off rocky, she was about to be a grandmother, Kristian was missing, and her eldest son was stealing employees from his father. "Of course, he does," she said, sarcastically. "Who else would he pick?"

Gully shot her a glance yet he didn't reply. He didn't speak again until they were at the restaurant. "We're here," he announced. "You know the drill."

"Yeah, yeah, yeah," Carmen muttered. "I walk in front. You walk behind me." She smiled at the thought as she approached Cipriani's. While she hoped King was inside, her son was never punctual. Hence the reason she went ahead and got a table. He didn't show until 1:10, dressed in his usual attire, a suit from the *King* collection. "I swear. You're going to be late to your own funeral."

"I've been busy," he blurted, plopping down in his seat. "You know about the deal." King dropped his cell phone on the table in case he got any calls. He couldn't afford to lose time so he had to multitask even if it meant he was distracted during lunch. "I'm trying to rent office space in a building downtown. Hopefully, I can get four floors. I'm looking to invest in a studio and I also had an interview with Vlad. I got a lot going on."

"I know you do," Carmen revealed. "But even with all you got going on; you still find time to be a man." A confused look appeared on his face so she explained. "Coco stopped by my office this morning. We talked for a few. I invited her to lunch, but she sent me an email and told me she wasn't coming. She did ask me to share some information with you."

"I talk to my girl every day. What are you gonna tell me that she couldn't?"

Carmen didn't bother to hold back. "She's pregnant." Carmen had already pictured the face he was going to make and even the words he might say. However, she didn't expect for him to get up from the table. "Where are you going? We need to talk about this."

"I need to talk to her. She should've told me first. This is our situation."

"Sit down," Carmen ordered. "You're not leaving this restaurant until we both have a clear understanding of how you're going to deal with this."

King's forehead furrowed at her words as he sat down. "What do you mean how I'm gonna deal with this? I'm not shocked that she's pregnant. I know what I did. Now with a baby on the way, we can get married."

Once again, Carmen's hands were covering her face. Her son was openly admitting the pregnancy was planned, or at least on his part. "What are you doing? You quit working for Jay. You're starting a record label, becoming a father, and a husband, all in the same year?"

"I'm doing the same shit you did, Mother."

If she wasn't trying to be civil, she would've cursed him. Then again, her son was right. She became a CEO, birthed him, and married his stepfather, Kane, all in the same year. Not to mention, she was only a year or two older than him when she did it. "I want you to be better than me. I set you up so you could. You're now a twenty year-old mogul and you can't even legally drink."

"Sounds like I was raised well," King fired back. "I can take care of my kid. Shit, I've been taking care of Malachi. When was the last time you got a call from the school? He's stayed on the high honor roll. He doesn't want for nothing. I'm not a good big brother; I'm a damn good father."

"I guess I gave you the perfect person to practice on," Carmen replied.

"I did the same."

Carmen turned to her left to see Jay standing beside her. He was the last person she expected to see at Cipriani's. She watched as he grabbed a chair from another table. "What are you doing here?" she quipped. "I didn't tell you about lunch."

"You didn't have to. Gully did." Jay didn't hesitate to turn his attention to King. "What is this shit you're trying to pull? I know all about you asking Malik and Nicholas to work for you."

Carmen knew the conversation was going nowhere with Jay at the table. His tone was monstrous, which King didn't want to hear. Food wasn't even on the table and her son was standing up again like he didn't plan on eating. "Well, that went well," she whispered once King walked away. She reached for her glass until she noticed King's phone. She immediately grabbed it only because she knew he was coming back for it.

"Can you believe he asked Malik to be Vice President?"

Carmen rolled her eyes because there were bigger issues on the table than Malik's employment. King hadn't returned so she didn't know whether to tell Jay he was going to be a grandfather now or when their son came back. She also needed to tell him about her meeting with their wedding planners and Kristian. Still debating, she decided to tell him about his future stepdaughter. "Kane called this morning. Apparently, Kristian is missing again."

"Where did she go?" Jay's voice was nonchalant only because he didn't know the severity of the situation. When Carmen didn't speak, he looked at her only to catch a side eye. "Don't look at me like that. Am I supposed to know where she went?"

"She's missing. We don't know where she went. Kane thinks she went to see Victor. However, I won't ask your opinion because I can tell this is the farthest thing from your mind. All you care about is this damn record label. You didn't even ask about my meeting with Patience and Veronica." Carmen stood up, ready to end the conversation. When Jay did the same, she knew they were about to have their own spat.

"This record label affects all my shit," he shot back. "What do you think is going to happen when Malik becomes VP? Who is going to manage Sapphire if Nicholas is scouting for talent all fuckin' day? You act like you don't care about my shit crumbling."

"I do care," Carmen yelled, pointing her finger at him. "But my daughter is missing *again*. I also had to sit in a meeting about *our* wedding by myself."

"Kristian has been begging to go to Georgia for months. This disappearance isn't a surprise. And why are you bringing up this meeting? Our wedding is a year from now. There will be plenty more. This stunt with King is different. I have to deal with this now."

Carmen took a deep breath as people stared in their direction. Not to mention, she saw King coming towards them. "Look, I know we have time on the wedding and I know this record label has you upset; however, right now, King needs this. I'm not saying he's right, because he's not, but he is going to need a lot of help. He's going to be a father. Coco is pregnant."

Jay wasn't quite sure how to react to the bomb Carmen dropped. He stood still for what felt like the longest until he saw King standing beside him. His son reached for his phone, which Carmen didn't immediately hand over. Jay was glad she didn't and used the time to his advantage. "The last thing you're gonna have people thinking is that all we do is drop babies. I made enough kids for both of us. You're not about to do the same. You're supposed to be better than me."

King narrowed his eyes, realizing his mother told him about Coco's pregnancy. His father may have thought he was following in his footsteps, but he wasn't. "I am better than you. Coco and I are already engaged. As soon as Mama hands me my phone, I can get our minister on the line. From the way I see it, I'll be married before you."

Carmen grabbed Jay's arm when she saw him lunge at King. She held him in place while her free hand gave King his phone. The quicker she could get him away from the table, the easier it would be to calm Jay down. Or so she thought. King's words only made Jay turn on her.

"Get your fuckin' divorce."

His tone was fiery, filled with as much angst as his attitude. Carmen would've replied the same if he wasn't leaving the table. Although he was walking away, the conversation wasn't over. He was bound to come home, which meant they would duke it out then. In the meantime, she accepted that lunch was over. She quickly grabbed her things and dropped a hundred dollar bill on the table for her drink and the chaos.

"That's the bullshit I didn't want to deal with," Gully said once they were in the limo. "You can't even have a civil conversation without someone wanting to lay hands."

About to comment, Carmen was interrupted by an incoming call from Kane. She answered rather quickly, hoping he had an update on Kristian.

"I got a hold of her," he disclosed. "She's in Georgia. She isn't with Victor yet, but that's who she's there to see. Right now, she's trying to rent a car."

"Trying to rent a car my ass," Carmen yelled. "When you get there, I want you to whoop her ass for me and you. This girl is about to give me a damn heart attack." Carmen waited impatiently for a response. "Did you hear me?"

"I'm not going to Georgia."

"What do you mean you're not going?"

"Kristian is fine. She wants to see about Victor, so let her. She feels indebted to him. In her mind, he's her hero."

"Shit, I'm her fuckin' hero. I was the one who killed Blu. I'm also yours. I just gave you a job and three thousand dollars. What the fuck are you doing with my money?" Carmen listened as Gully honked the horn. She thought it was for her expletives until she noticed the traffic. "I gave you that money to help you get to Georgia. If you're not going, you need to give it back."

"I'll give it back. Damn. You act like I robbed you. It's not like you need the money. Three thousand is probably lunch money to you. Besides, Kristian is only one of the reasons I'm not going," Kane explained. "The other reason is King. He just called me. He told me about his situation with Coco. He also told me about this dinner with you and her parents. He said Coco texted him about it. He wants me to come for support. You know he still sees me as his father. I did raise him for seventeen years."

Carmen dropped the phone only because things were getting worse. She couldn't care less about the petty cash she gave him when there was about to be an all-out brawl in her dining room. She hadn't mentioned the dinner to Jay so when he saw Kane in the house, he was definitely going to flip. *I know King did this on purpose. He keeps poking the bear like he wants Jay to bite.*

"When do you want me to start work?" Kane asked, interrupting her thoughts. "Oh, do you want me and Monifah to bring something for dinner?"

Carmen picked up her phone, hearing his voice. "You can start next week once your background check comes in. And, didn't you tell me that you and Monifah were through?"

"Well, we were," Kane chuckled, "until she came over and fucked me like a wildebeest. I wouldn't be getting any if it wasn't for her. It's not like I can sleep with you. Or can I? We actually should have one more night together before the divorce is final."

Carmen immediately hung up the phone. The closest Kane would ever get to being in between her legs was in his dreams. Their time had passed and they both knew it. Too angry to even curse, she watched as Gully pulled in front of Flame. She didn't get out, choosing to sit there quietly as she tried to tame her anger. Thankfully, Gully let her be until she decided to go inside. When she exited the car, he told her to have a good day only to get a middle finger in return. It gave him a chuckle, a sound she heard until she was away from the vehicle.

The first place she went was to her office since there weren't any other meetings lined up. With time to herself, she could figure out dinner and decide what she was going to do about Kristian. Dinner, much simpler to deal with, only required a phone call home to Fiona. Once her maid had a meal planned, she put in a call to Kristian, not to yell and scream, but to be the concerned parent she was. When Kristian didn't answer, a part of her wasn't surprised. Her daughter probably thought checking in with her father was good enough. *It doesn't matter the reason*, Carmen thought. *I'm going to keep calling until I get her. She has to know this isn't acceptable. She wants to be grown so bad, but she has so much more living to do.*

4

The Crying Game

Almost six-thirty, Carmen walked in her home only to be met with the smell of Parmesan, a result of Fiona's cooking. She stood in the doorway of the dining room to find the table already set. Not quite sure what was left to do, she placed her tote bag in the home office before heading in the kitchen. She expected to see Fiona, but instead found Jay.

"Where's Fiona?" she asked, taking a seat on one of the bar stools.

"She went to pick up a cake," he replied. "We're supposedly having some special dinner."

Carmen placed her left palm over her forehead suddenly remembering she never mentioned it to him. "I am so sorry," she apologized. "Today has been crazy. I meant to tell you earlier. The Mastersons are going to be joining us. King also invited Kane and Mo—"

The kitchen door swung open, interrupting her. Fiona entered the kitchen, announcing Maya's arrival, which made Carmen look to Jay for approval.

"You really wanna have this dinner when I'm at war with King?" Jay wasn't looking for a way out because he knew the dinner was going to happen regardless. "It doesn't matter. You already got everything in motion. I won't bring up the label as long as he doesn't."

Carmen whispered thank you, which was enough to end the discussion. Jay left the room to check on Rakim and Nyla while she headed towards the front door to greet Maya. Once in the foyer, Carmen opened the door only to hear someone coming down the steps. Maya was still getting out the car so Carmen looked behind her to see Akaila, the adopted daughter she shared with Kane. She lived with Carmen and Jay while her biological brother, Malachi, lived with King.

"There's a face I haven't seen all day," Carmen gushed. She gave her a big smile only for it not to be returned. "Don't tell me something is wrong with you, too."

"I just got off the phone with Kristian. She's in Georgia," Akaila replied.

"I found that out this morning." Carmen shook her head before turning towards the doorway. King and Coco were pulling up behind Maya, but Kane and Monifah had yet to arrive.

"I think she has a crush on Victor."

Carmen almost let the door close in Maya's face at Akaila's revelation. Quickly grabbing it, she opened it wider so Maya could walk in. "What makes you think that?"

"Did I arrive at a bad time?" Maya interjected.

Carmen was about to say no until she saw Akaila look at her feet. It was obvious her daughter knew something she didn't. After telling Akaila they would discuss it later, she turned to address Maya. "You didn't arrive at a bad time. In fact, I'm glad you were punctual."

"I'm always punctual," Maya joked. "My husband asked me to apologize on his behalf. He won't be joining us tonight. You know how it is when work calls."

"We always take rain checks," Carmen replied. "Hopefully, he'll make the next one." She led Maya to the dining room where they found Fiona setting baskets of croissants on the table. King and Coco joined them a few minutes later, which was when Carmen learned Malachi was skipping out as well. She also found out from Jay, when he returned, that her mother, Patricia, wouldn't be joining them either. Instead, she opted to spend the evening caring for Rakim and Nyla.

Carmen didn't bother to question why, brushing the issue aside. She simply did a quick scan of the room to make sure everyone else was there as Jay took his usual seat at the head. King sat to the right of him, directly across from her while Coco sat next to her mother. Kane arrived alone, giving a random excuse for Monifah's absence. He sat at the opposite end of the table, at the head as well, creating an awkward arrangement. To add to the awkwardness, Maya encouraged him to bless the food. After he finished, she began her interrogation.

"There's no need to keep me waiting. It's not every day I'm invited over for dinner. Who do I owe this wondrous occasion? I see the whole family is here. Is there some big announcement other than King Records? Spill it. I'm ready for it."

Carmen intentionally chose not to speak. It wasn't her place to tell Maya her daughter was pregnant, so she decided to let someone else do the honor. She expected it to be Coco yet her lips remained sealed. In fact, no one spoke.

"So is this really happening?" Maya probed. "No one is going to say anything."

"We want to get married." King blurted the words, becoming somewhat comfortable since one of the secrets was out. "We've already spoken to Bro. Harrison who agreed to marry us as long as we attend some counseling sessions."

"So you got our minister to agree to marry you before you asked for my blessing?" Maya raised her voice, now offended. "Months ago, she started wearing a promise ring. Now, it's an engagement ring. Let me guess, the wedding is in two weeks."

"We want to do it December 31ˢᵗ," King dispelled. "You're right, I didn't ask for your blessing, which is why you're here. I need your blessing. Also, just so you know, she never had a promise ring. It was always an engagement ring."

Maya sighed. "You've made a big improvement, King. I will give you that. You're also financially stable. I don't question whether or not you can take care of her or if you'll be faithful. What I question is your lifestyle. You can't walk out the door without a weapon on you. Men have to follow you around because your last name alone makes people want to shoot you. I'm still distraught over what happened to Kristian. It could've been my child."

"Tread softly," Carmen interrupted.

"I'm only expressing the concerns *any* parent would have. I can look at the news and see it isn't easy being a Santiago. I also know from my daughter's experience, it's not easy to date one. God bless the souls of those who married one." The sound of Jay's chair moving silenced Maya, but only temporarily. Despite everyone's expectation, he didn't get up, but he made Maya conscience of her words. "All I'm saying," she continued. "Is that I have reservations."

"We're getting married," King pressed. "We don't need your blessing to do it."

"You're right, you don't," Maya shot back, "but shouldn't you want it? Isn't it important?"

King took his time answering. While tradition said he needed it, he believed he didn't. Nonetheless, Maya didn't want his personal beliefs. She wanted a politically correct answer. "Very important," he lied.

The words, "I'm glad," served as Maya's only response. She didn't elaborate, leaving everyone unsure of her stance. In Carmen's opinion, it was a ploy to halt their plans or to buy some time to think things over. *Her opinion doesn't matter*, Carmen thought, *King is going to move forward with this wedding regardless*. A true statement, Carmen listened as King began to share his ideas for his nuptials. The discussion was lengthy and somehow both he and Coco left the dinner table without ever mentioning the pregnancy. It was like they had purposely skipped the subject. Carmen was certain Maya would find out later until they were in the foyer having small talk. Most of the conversation was playful until Maya's tone unexpectedly became serious.

"I've watched the things you've been through," she began, her voice coming out in a rattle. "I know you and Jay have things together now, but I remember when y'all were on that rocky road. I don't want that for my daughter. I also don't want her to settle down before she has the chance to fully enjoy her youth." Tears formed in Maya's eyes eventually falling down her face. "She made her bed, though, and, now she has to lie in it. I'll be damned if she brings a bastard in this world. If that means she has to marry King then so be it."

Carmen froze solid. For most of the evening she wondered when Coco's pregnancy would be disclosed. It never happened and now it didn't matter because Maya used her own intuition to put two and two together. Her words stung because it reminded Carmen of her mother's attitude when she discovered she was pregnant with King. To silence any speculation, she was pressured to become legally married prior to her son's birth. She tied the knot with Kane while Jay was in prison and raised King to believe that Kane was his biological father. Coco's experience was slightly different, but it didn't mean her transition would be easy.

"They're in love," was all Carmen could say.

"She doesn't know what love is. She's a child, a baby."

Maya wiped her face, but it was pointless. The tears were still falling as she came to grips that her daughter was pregnant. "He better not hurt her. If King breaks her heart, I will kill him. You hear me, Carmen? I will kill him."

Carmen clenched her jaw as a sign to Maya her words didn't fall on deaf ears. She paid the threat no mind because she was confident in her son's relationship. Maya may not have been, but time would certainly prove her wrong. "Have a good night, Maya. I highly suggest you have a conversation with Coco when you get home." Maya looked at her dumbfounded. Her words, obviously offensive, sent Maya rushing out the front door. She watched her as she got in her vehicle and once she was out the driveway, she slammed the door shut.

5

Only

After her emotional conversation with Maya, Carmen escaped to the kitchen to have some time alone. Fiona had cleaned the kitchen prior to leaving for the night so there was little to do except unload the dishwasher. A job that took less than twenty minutes, Carmen stretched it into forty. She moved slowly, ignoring the clock until her moment of peace was disturbed.

"Well, it's quiet down here," her mother, Patricia, said as she dropped an empty glass on the counter. "I guess the kitchen is safe now." She chuckled for a bit until she realized her daughter wasn't smiling. "Maybe, it isn't."

Carmen set the plate she was holding inside the cabinet once she saw it shake in her hand. Her mother's presence was only a reminder of the stunt she pulled at dinner. Her absence was not only rude to their guests, but also uncalled for. "Did something happen that I don't know about?"

Patricia groaned in annoyance at Carmen's question. She didn't think her absence was a big deal considering she didn't fare well with Jay. If anything, she was keeping the peace by remaining upstairs. "I try to limit my contact with your fiancé. Besides, I already know about King's shotgun wedding. It's a shame the things we have to do to cover up sin."

Carmen stared at her mother in complete disgust. Her words were merely reminiscent of the speech she gave her nearly twenty years ago when she discovered her pregnancy. "They were already planning on getting married," Carmen explained. "The pregnancy was a bonus. No, the conception was not right, but this is not something anyone should hold over their heads. We've all made mistakes."

"Yes, we have, but this isn't something to be proud of. That girl is only eighteen. What was King thinking? Y'all didn't teach him about using condoms? Wait, don't answer that. I know you didn't. You barely use them."

Carmen's eyes narrowed at her mother's insult. She could feel a slew of expletives on the tip of her tongue yet her mother exited before the words could be spewed. The idea to follow her remained constant until her mother's footsteps could no longer be heard. Then, as if her mother wanted her to know she was upset, she slammed her bedroom door closed. Ignoring her tantrum, Carmen left the kitchen and headed straight to her bedroom. Jay was already inside, changing out his slacks into a pair of sweatpants.

"Let me guess, you're the reason she slammed the door."

Carmen rubbed her brow as a way to illustrate that her mother was giving her a headache. "She's got so much to say like she's never made a mistake. She and Maya are one in the same. They're so concerned about protecting their images they don't see its ruining their relationships." A small sigh escaped her lips as she reached out for him. "Hold me, please."

Jay did as she asked, allowing her to rest her head on his chest. For at least five minutes, she wanted to think of completely nothing. Her wish was granted until she heard her phone ring.

Carmen picked her phone up once she saw *Kristian* flashing on the screen. She had waited for hours to hear from her daughter so her conversation with Jay was about to take a backseat. Not to mention, she needed to talk to her about Victor. "So you're just now returning my call," she blurted, heading towards her walk-in closet. "What have you been doing for the last four to six hours?"

"I'm at Victor's. My phone was on silent. I was calling to let you know I'm all right. I talked to Daddy earlier. Did he tell you he talked to me?"

Carmen rolled her eyes at her daughter's insensitivity. "Just because you live with your father doesn't mean he's your only parent. Yeah, he told me, but you should've called me, too. I was worried out my damn mind when he told me you were missing."

Kristian knew she had kept her mother out the loop. However, she didn't expect her to worry like she had. "I'm sorry he scared you. I'm also sorry I didn't tell you about the trip. Every time I asked about going, you always said no. I knew if I asked again, you would say the same thing. I know I'm in trouble and I'll accept my punishment when I get back."

Carmen took a deep breath. "You are in trouble. You're also grounded and I have every intention of putting my foot up your ass when you come home. I'm fine with you staying, but only for one night. I want you home tomorrow. I don't know anything about this Victor guy so you need to be on the first flight out."

"Well, if it helps, Victor actually wants to talk to you."

A look of surprise flew across Carmen's face. She was going to demand to speak to him, but now she didn't have to. "The feeling is mutual. Put him on the phone."

"He wants you to know he didn't have anything to do with me coming out here," Kristian explained. "I'm gonna give you to him." She handed the phone to Victor.

"Good evening, Ms. Davenport," Victor greeted. "How are you?"

Carmen answered with a quick, "fine," as Jay joined her in the closet. He didn't say anything to her, simply standing there and listening to the conversation. "Are you taking care of my baby?"

"I am," Victor replied. "I wanted to speak with you to let you know her visit was a surprise. I didn't know she was coming. I actually didn't expect to see her until my court date."

"And when is that?" Carmen asked. Victor responded to her, but Carmen didn't catch his reply. Her eyes were once again on Jay who was dissecting her every move. "I'm sorry, Victor. When did you say your trial was?" He repeated his answer, but Carmen still didn't hear him.

Despite his lack of words, Jay was adamant about getting her attention. Victor was still speaking, but Carmen only caught bits and pieces. Within the last thirty seconds or so, the imprint of Jay's love muscle had become visible. It caught her off guard to the point she ignored every word Victor said.

"Kristian has told us a lot about you," she said, turning away. "I think it's time we meet. I need to see who this Victor Fontaine is."

"Yes, once everything blows over," Victor agreed. "I don't mind traveling to New York. I actually need a vacation. It has been really hard living—" Victor stopped speaking when the line went dead. Unsure if the phone lost signal, he pulled it from his ear to see the words, *Call Ended*. He looked at Kristian questionably. "I don't know what happened."

Kristian grabbed the phone, but *Mom* was long gone from the screen. "Did she hang up? Her phone could've died. Maybe she lost signal."

Victor shrugged his shoulders. "She was saying she wanted us to meet for lunch and then it just went dead. I didn't hear anybody in the background. It didn't sound like she was driving."

Kristian twisted her mouth. When a minute passed and her mother hadn't called back, she decided not to linger on the issue. "Well, at least you talked to her. If she offered to meet you then she doesn't see you as a threat."

"I never was a threat." Victor stood up from the couch now somewhat comfortable after his brief conversation with Carmen. He was still trying to clear his name and wanted her to know her daughter's latest stunt wasn't his doing. From the way Carmen spoke, she obviously believed him.

Victor was set on seeing after Kristian even if it was only for twenty-four hours. To prove it, he headed to his guestroom to make sure the area was presentable. Only days since his release from jail, he hadn't ventured in the room in months. Due to his violent confrontation with Blu's goons during her kidnapping, the room along with other parts of his apartment had been ransacked. Then, it became a part of the investigation so there were more strange hands on his property. If it wasn't for his mother, he would've been released from jail to find his things boxed up in her attic or in storage. Thankfully, during his hospitalization, his mother was able to take control of his estate. She even appealed his eviction so he was able to keep a roof over his head.

From the looks of things, his mother did a good job of putting his apartment back together. Still, he continued to inspect the area while Kristian retrieved her belongings from her car. When she returned to the apartment, Victor retired to his room so she could get settled. He washed the day off and ten minutes later, he was in bed, clad only in his boxers.

Hours passed, allowing him to fall in a deep state of unconsciousness. Once there, he was met with a vivid image of Kristian. In fact, he almost felt as if she was right in front of him. He saw her clearly, standing at the foot of his bed, her arms draped at her side. He asked her if everything was okay, a question which didn't generate a verbal response. Instead, Kristian crawled on the bed until she was hovering over him. Victor swallowed, realizing he was right between her legs. Although she was fully clothed, the closeness of her body enticed him. It also made him nervous. Months since he'd been intimate, his appetite for sex was extremely high.

"We can't do this," he told her. She hadn't moved, her body still frozen on top of his, but he'd already read her mind. Kristian wanted him inside of her and deep down he wanted the same. Throughout his stay in the hospital, they kept in frequent contact. The long hours they spent conversing allowed him to get to know her way beyond the physical. He shunned his feelings for the longest, telling himself he was too old, and to be with her was too dangerous. Nevertheless, he fed himself lies. None of those were factors, only excuses. Ready to give in, he parted his lips only to see her fade.

Victor's eyes opened, quickly adjusting to the darkness. Kristian wasn't in his room, merely a figment of his imagination, but her voice, now a series of shrill screams was ever present. Automatically, his hand went underneath his pillow, wrapping around a recently purchased 357 Magnum. A firm grip was on the gun as he ran to the guestroom, her screams even louder as he approached. Her door was still closed and when he opened it, he found her inside alone. He didn't drop the gun, staring at her as she shook in the bed until his presence woke her. *A nightmare*, he thought as she sat up. When she finally caught her breath, he closed the bedroom door.

Unlike in *his* dream, he was at the foot of her bed. He stayed there for a minute or so as she gathered herself before moving closer. Once at the head, he set the gun on the left bedside dresser. He then pulled the covers back so he could slide in next to her. When she didn't voice her displeasure, his own reservations were forgotten. He pulled her into him until her head rested on his chest. "I got you," he whispered. To further reiterate his words, he slid his hand in her hair. He softly massaged her scalp, calming her until she fell asleep.

6

Hold Up

Carmen awoke to find herself in a similar position as Victor and Kristian. The only difference was that she was lying nude on the floor of her walk-in closet. She reminded herself to never have sex there again. Her back was sore from the floor and she suspected she may have carpet burn on her right leg.

Despite the heaviness of her eyes, she still got up. She showered and dressed in under forty minutes leaving her plenty of time to head to Rakim's room. To her surprise, Nyla was asleep beside him. They were both still resting so she stood there quietly in hopes they would wake. When they didn't, she softly kissed their cheeks and tiptoed out the room.

Only a few minutes were left to spare so she made a final pit stop in her bedroom. Jay was now awake, standing naked in the closet, sorting through his suits. "Gully is downstairs," she announced, grabbing her purse from the bed. "I'm getting ready to head out." She walked in the closet as he grabbed a pair of khaki pants. A small kiss followed, which led Jay to wrap his hands around her waist. He gave it a tight squeeze almost as if he was ready to start round two. "Unh-uh," she told him, moving his hands. "Last night has to hold you for a while."

As if extra help was needed to stop another escapade, Nyla's cries sounded from the baby monitor. Jay pulled away, well aware it was time for daddy duty. Nyla was only getting louder and he needed to get to her before she woke up the rest of the house. He moved quickly, grabbing a pair of boxers and sweatpants, which he slid on before running out the room.

In the meantime, Carmen headed downstairs and out the door. Gully was already waiting in the car with the engine running. "Good morning," she greeted, sliding in the backseat.

Gully glanced at her through the rearview mirror. Her voice sounded peppy yet her eyes were already closing as if she hadn't gotten enough rest. "Good morning to you, too," he replied. He cracked a smile when she didn't respond, a sign she was indeed knocked out. The ride to Flame wasn't a long one, but she was able to fall in a deep slumber. He honked the horn to wake her when his voice didn't do the job. Once she stirred, he unlocked the doors. "I'm going to assume you were up all night wedding planning," he joked. "I'll drive by around lunchtime. If you need me before then, let me know."

"Cool." Carmen yawned, opening the door. She stepped out the car, still wearing the effects of sleep. The trek to her office took longer than usual, but she made it onto the executive floor by eight-thirty. Certain Cathy had a to-do list for her, she was surprised when her receptionist didn't follow her to her office. Cathy remained at her desk as if they didn't have an agenda. Since she had, Carmen closed her door and sat at her desk, automatically falling asleep.

Not quite sure how long she was out, she woke up from her nap to be met with an incoming call from her lawyer, Clement. Her counsel for the past twenty or so years, he was responsible for seeing her through every legal aspect of her life, from business to divorce. He was also King's lawyer and despite confidentiality, he would always give her the heads up on whatever her son had brewing. "This better be good," she told him as she wiped sleep from her eyes. "I hope this call isn't about King Records."

"This is good," Clement reiterated. "Your divorce was finalized this morning."

Carmen closed her eyes only because Clement's words reminded her of what Jay had said at lunch the other day. His words, *Get your fuckin' divorce*, seemed to echo all around her. She could now tell him it was done. You're my favorite person right now."

"I got the paperwork this morning. I'll have one of my couriers drop it off. I know Jay is going to be happy."

"He is. It's been a long time coming."

"I know it has. I wish you two the best. I'm looking forward to the wedding."

"Make that two of us." Carmen grinned at the thought as Clement asked about the wedding plans. Not much had been done, but Carmen gave him a few minor details before the call ended. As much as she wanted to call Jay with the news, she decided to wait until the papers were in her hands. She wanted physical proof she was legally free to become Carmen Denise Santiago. Jay would take her word for it regardless, but the news would be more momentous if he saw the signed paperwork. Unsure of when it would be delivered, Carmen planned to tell him after dinner. They could take a walk around the estate and when he least expected it, she would surprise him with the news.

"You look happy," a voice said, interrupting her thoughts.

Carmen looked up to see King standing in the doorway. She hadn't heard her door open nor did she expect to get a visit from him. "I wasn't expecting you. I thought you had your hands full with a wedding and a baby."

"I do. That's why I came by. I need to go over some wedding stuff."

Carmen raised her brow because she knew King was going to ask for a favor. While she hoped it was monetary, something told her it wasn't. "Let me have it. It can't be that bad. Today is starting off better than yesterday." Carmen watched as King placed several papers on her desk. Scribbled handwriting lined the pages as well as terrible sketches of dresses and suits. She automatically thought the worst, assuming he wanted her to design outfits for the wedding party. Thankfully, he didn't mention it.

"I stopped by to talk about the wedding party. Coco and I finalized the details last night. It was harder than I thought because I couldn't find a best man. I asked Malachi, but he's worried about holding onto the ring. Nicholas and I are still rebuilding our friendship. Phase is swamped with stuff at Sapphire. Malik has too much on his plate. I feel like I have no choice, but to ask my father."

"Wow," Carmen mouthed. "That's a step in the right direction."

King knew his mother thought he was speaking of Jay. While he was his biological father, he wasn't the one who raised him. In his mind, Kane was his father and Jay was simply a former employer with a few father-like qualities. He hadn't planned on Jay doing anything aside from helping with the rings, reception, and honeymoon. "I'm talking about Kane," he explained. "Jay isn't in the wedding. Malik, Nicholas, and Phase are groomsmen while I figured Linx, Roman, and Gully would handle security."

Carmen's facial expression became blank at King's decision. She understood why he chose Kane, but she thought the wedding and Coco's pregnancy were perfect reasons for him to mend his relationship with Jay. King was legally a Santiago, making Coco one and also bringing a baby into the world who would carry the same last name. "At some point in time you and Jay have to get over this hump," she began. "I will never take anything away from your stepfather. He did an amazing job raising you, but you can't be mad at Jay forever. He wants to work things out while you want to hold a grudge. If you give Kane this, you and Jay can't reconcile. It will hurt him to his core."

Carmen didn't allow him to respond, choosing to remind him of their past relationship. "You and Jay used to be close. Before you found out he was your father, you were with him every day. Y'all lived together. Your relationship didn't change until..." Carmen realized the root of the problem. "Your relationship changed when I got pregnant with Rakim. That's what made you angry. You wanted Jay all to yourself. You're upset with him, but you really need to be mad at me. Jay didn't create Rakim by himself."

King didn't respond, starting to sort through the papers he placed on his mother's desk. His mother was right, but he didn't want to admit it. He'd been jealous of his little brother since his conception. The experiences Rakim had with their father were ones he could only dream about. He also believed Rakim was his father's favorite.

"Don't do this to him," Carmen begged. "You know the history between him and Kane. Your stepfather will always be a sensitive topic because of what I did. I have to live with it, but you don't. Give Jay the job. If you ask me, he probably thinks Malachi is going to be your best man. Once he learns its Kane, it's going to tear him apart. He's missed so many of your milestones; you could at least give him this one. Or you can look at it like this. This wedding is the starting point of y'all ending this war. Tell Jay you're making amends. Start fresh. I mean, you have to walk me down the aisle to him next year. Go ahead and get on a clean page now."

"I want Rakim to be the ring bearer," King announced, not bothering to address what she said. "I wish Nyla was old enough to walk down the aisle. Since she can't, the Goggins' little girls will serve as flower girls. Kristian will be Coco's maid of honor while one of her aunts is going to be her matron of honor."

Carmen grabbed King's papers in case he used the documents to stall. "Don't ignore me. This is serious. If you make Kane your best man, when Jay comes to the wedding, it will end your relationship with him. If you don't want Jay to be your best man then give the job to Malachi or Nicholas. Just don't give it to Kane."

"You act like I'm doing this to make him mad."

The words, "because you are," were thunderous out Carmen's mouth. "It's the same shit you're pulling with this record label. You're mad at Jay for a lot of things, and you want revenge. Okay, I get it, you're upset, you're angry, but when does it stop? Jay isn't the one keeping this thing going, it's you. You're the one being stubborn. You hate Jay so much, but I bet you talk to him more than Kane."

King didn't speak yet he held out his hands as a sign he was ready to leave. Carmen didn't immediately hand the papers over until King rose from his seat. Certain his mind was made up, she gave him the papers, allowing him to leave her office. There was nothing more she could say or do to fix his relationship with Jay. While she hated to give up, King didn't leave her much of a choice. If he made Kane his best man, she would never get in the middle again. All she could do was pray. If he didn't change his mind come the day of his wedding, Jay would consider him a Santiago only by name.

7

Daddy Lessons

King's meeting with Carmen went unknown to Jay as he walked inside the poorly lit diner. A place he hadn't frequented in ages, he invited King there on purpose. The diner, still located in West Brookstone, was where he first met Carmen. With his son set to tie the knot in a few weeks, he needed to smooth over the tension between them. He wasn't quite sure how receptive King would be, but it was worth a shot. If anything, he hoped the conversation remained cordial.

King arrived minutes later, his face wearing a clear expression of surprise. "I wasn't expecting this," he voiced. "Not after what happened at Cipriani's." King would admit his conversation with his mother had sparked something in him. Still, it wasn't enough for him to invite his father to breakfast. Obviously, there was something weighing on Jay's mind, which made him make the call. "Maybe, deep down, we both knew this was needed."

Jay gazed at his son from all angles to make sure it was him. After spending countless months arguing over their businesses, Kristian, and whatever else they thought was debatable, he often lost hope in saving their relationship. Now, King spoke as if they had a chance. "You're still my son regardless of what differences we have. You're also about to be a husband *and* a father. Neither is going to be easy. Are you ready to commit to one woman?"

King cracked a smile. To him, being faithful wasn't a challenge. He loved Coco too much to risk losing her. "You don't want anyone else when one woman gives you everything. Isn't it like that with my mom? Are you ready to commit to one woman?" King was quick to remind his father of his own nuptials.

"I committed to one woman the day I saw your mother in this diner." Jay pointed to his left to show King the booth he was sitting in. "I brought you here for breakfast because this is where I met your mother. Twenty years ago, I was sitting right there. It was me, Carlos, my best friend at the time who you never met, Malik, and his twin brother, Rakim. That's who your little brother is named after. We were here for about thirty minutes before your mother walked in with Tiara and sat in this very booth." Jay pointed at the table where they were sitting. "I couldn't take my eyes off her."

"The rest is history," King said with a laugh.

"The rest *is* history," Jay repeated. "Ever since that day, we were together. We had our ups and downs like we still do, but I couldn't let her go. As you can see, she couldn't let me go either. You need to have that same kind of love when it comes to Coco. You can commit to one woman when she completes you."

King nodded his head in agreement. The waitress was returning with their drinks so he didn't voice his thought until after they had placed their orders. When she left their table, he noticed his father appeared somewhat uneasy. "What's on your mind?"

"When was the last time we did this? Lately, all we do is fight. If we're not fighting, we're ignoring each other."

King shrugged his shoulders. "Probably before Rakim was born. Things were different then. When Rakim came along, I feel like a lot changed. You ask me all the time what the problem is and I never give you an answer. Maybe, I wasn't quite sure what it was. I think I've figured it out now." King paused for a bit only to catch his breath. "I had to live without you. I don't think it's fair. The decision was made for me. The decision was almost made for Rakim, but you fought for him. Why didn't you fight for me?"

"I was sick." Jay looked his son square in the eye when he said the words. "Everything was being stripped of me. I found out your mother was pregnant when I was being arrested. I had a life sentence hanging over my head. In a way, I thought I was making the best decision. What's the point of reaching out if you couldn't see me? That was my mindset. I became content with it and after seventeen years, I got an offer I couldn't refuse. I came home with the intention of reclaiming everything that was mine."

"And you did," King replied. "You had me, you had my mom. But that wasn't enough for you. So you went and made Rakim. He's getting everything I should've got from you."

Jay placed both his arms on the table. Not quite sure how to respond, he remained silent until the words came to him. "I understand why you feel that way. The time I'm getting with Rakim is the time I lost with you. It wasn't easy getting out of prison and coming home to a son who is already seventeen. Now, you're twenty, and it's still hard. Rakim calls me Daddy, you call me Jay."

King knew his father was right. For most of his life, Kane had been Daddy. To even refer to Jay as such seemed awkward. "That's going to take time," he admitted. "I spent seventeen years of my life believing another man was my father. I'm not saying it's not going to happen, but it's something I have to work on. What I do know is that my son or daughter can't come in this world with our relationship like this. It's not healthy. So, as of today, I want to start fresh. I'm willing to let bygones be bygones. Let's move forward."

"That's what I've always wanted to do."

Jay held out his hand to his son, but King didn't take it. "Is there something else?"

"I need you to agree to be my best man."

King's wedding party had been the furthest thing from Jay's mind. He overlooked it as his attention was drawn more towards King Records and Coco's pregnancy. Now that he did give it some thought, he understood why King wanted him to be the best man considering the responsibilities. However, he thought the role needed to go to Malachi. The two had been glued to the hip way before Malachi's adoption was complete. In a way, Malachi was more of a son to King than a brother.

"I can't shake on that," Jay stated, speaking his thoughts. "I understand why you're giving the role to me, but it's not mine. I really feel like Malachi should be your best man. Now, I'll help him with the bachelor party. I'll even glue the rings to his hands. But," he continued. "I don't need that title. I'm fine just being there and being your dad."

King became confused as his father turned down his request. After his conversation with his mother, she made him believe it was only right to give Jay the position. Now that he had, his father had declined. He started to persuade him to do otherwise until he was interrupted by their waitress. She set their plates in front of him and Jay proceeded to bless the food.

"You look like you were going to say something," Jay stated, after finishing the prayer.

"I was going to say I'm disappointed," King responded. "I thought this would be something you wanted." King watched as his father ate. Jay didn't look bothered by the conversation as if saying no was easy to do. "I know you don't want Kane to be my best man." A sudden change occurred in his father's demeanor. He actually froze. Jay's mood was enough to let King know the idea wasn't going to fly.

"I know all about the role Kane played in your life," Jay began. "I will never take away what he's done for you. He was your father when I couldn't be. What I will attack is his character. There's nothing authentic about him. He's like a bootleg. The things he's done to me, putting me in prison, stealing Carmen from me, changing paternity tests so he can claim Rakim as his son.

You shouldn't want him in your wedding. If you're giving me an ultimatum then my answer is yes. I'll be your best man. I just don't want it to be him."

King wanted to remind his father of his own shortcomings, but he chose not to. It wouldn't have aided their fresh start. Nevertheless, his mother already warned him about making Kane his best man. Jay's words only confirmed it. The best thing to do was honor his wishes. "I hear you. But, if it's something you really don't want then I'll get Malachi to do it."

"He's a good pick. He's been living with you all this time."

King laughed at the comment. "True. Well, now that my best man is taken care of, who is doing the honor at your wedding?"

"Malik," Jay revealed. "However, that may change if he quits on me." Jay cracked a smile only so King could see he was joking. "Malik and I talked briefly this morning. He explained to me that he's ready to have something of his own. Sapphire and Iceland are mine. Blue Magic is owned by me and your mom. While he won't have ownership in King Records, he thinks it can lead to something big. He wants to look into artist management."

"So he's taking the position?"

Jay shrugged his shoulders. "He's thinking about it. He has to see what the pay is going to be." Jay chuckled until a man standing outside the restaurant caught his eye. He was depositing change into a newspaper vending machine. Suddenly, he was reminded of Grendel's words. *'It would be to your benefit to pick up a newspaper. Educate yourself on blood diamonds. Find out as much as you can about your supplier. That's the best advice I can give you. Once you do, we can have another conversation."*

"One second," he told King, standing up. He quickly ventured outside just as the man closed the door to the vending machine. While it had been months since he purchased a paper, he quickly bought a copy of *The Brookstone Times*. He returned to the restaurant and while King ate, he scanned the pages of the newspaper until he reached the *World* section.

"What cha lookin' for?" King asked, noticing the paper in his father's hands.

"Something I heard about earlier," Jay answered. He moved his plate out the way so he could place the newspaper on the table. He continued scanning it until his eyes focused on a small headline in the bottom right-hand corner. *Torture, beatings, and murder*, it read. *Inside the new brutal 'blood diamonds' scandal.* Well aware this was the news Grendel wanted him to see, Jay pulled an ink pen out his pocket. He marked the article before folding the paper into its original shape. He then set it beside him in the booth.

"Well, did you find it?"

"Yeah," Jay voiced. "It was there. I'll read it later." He gave his son a small grin only because he didn't want King to become suspicious. Whatever was brewing with Grendel was a matter he wanted to keep private until he knew exactly what was going on. He also made the decision to get his diamonds out the states. His stones, once hidden in a tunnel underneath Flame, would soon be in a vault in the basement of his mansion in San Juan. The only jewels left in Brookstone would be pieces he planned to unveil at the grand opening of Iceland. In the event, he discovered he was part of the blood diamonds scandal, not only could Iceland come falling down, but his freedom could be threatened again.

8

I Lied

Carmen's eyes glanced at her door the moment she heard someone knock. Her attention immediately went to the email she received from Veronica confirming their next meeting. She forwarded the message to Jay as the person knocked again. Not wanting to be rude or to keep the person waiting, she gave them permission to enter. When Cathy walked in, Carmen immediately noticed the manila envelope in her hands.

"One of Clement's couriers dropped this off for you," her receptionist announced. "I know anything from his office is important."

"Majorly important," Carmen stressed. She was well aware of the envelope's contents. "I was expecting this," she said as she wandered over to the doorway. She slid the envelope from Cathy's hands, turning it over as if she could see through it. "I feel like I've been waiting on this forever." Carmen gazed at the envelope until she heard a new voice in the room. Looking up, the last person she expected to see at Flame was Kane.

Somewhat flabbergasted since the divorce papers were in her hand, Carmen didn't say a word. She assumed he came to discuss the divorce until she remembered she was his new employer. *How did I forget? He works here now. He came to talk about his new job.* About to speak, Carmen was silenced when Cathy excused herself. She closed the door behind her so Carmen headed to her desk where she slid the envelope inside her top drawer. She took her seat while Kane remained standing. "Was your paperwork good to go? The Human Resources department is on the seventh floor if you need to speak with them."

"I'm here to speak with you," Kane explained.

His tone, not the least bit cheerful, made Carmen rather nervous. Slowly, but surely, something was telling her he was there to discuss the divorce. "So you're here to talk to me. Go ahead. You have the floor."

"I got the papers today," Kane voiced. "Did you get 'em?"

Carmen let out a small breath only because Kane's words confirmed what she thought was true. In her opinion, they didn't have anything to discuss. They were divorced way before they received copies of the decree. "I got 'em," she told him, softly. "Is that what you came to talk about? You want to talk about the divorce?"

"Not so much," Kane replied. "That part is said and done."

Carmen became confused as to where Kane was taking the conversation. He asked about the papers, but at the same time, was saying he didn't come to discuss the divorce.

"We were married for twenty years," Kane continued. "Seven thousand and three hundred days, give or take. We talked about growing old together, having grandkids, even where we wanted to go on our fiftieth anniversary. I thought about that when I was staring at those papers. I even asked myself, 'Did I do everything possible to save my marriage?' I don't think I did." Kane rested his hands on her desk. "We both know I never wanted the divorce. I simply gave you what you wanted. If I made it seem like I did, well, I lied."

Carmen closed her eyes because Kane was leading the conversation in an area they didn't need to discuss. After a year of being separated, they both were in relationships with other people. She was certain they wouldn't be spending another afternoon going back and forth over the obvious. Especially not when she was engaged and he had a steady girlfriend.

"My feelings for Monifah are real. Maybe, that's the reason I was able to forgive her after she deceived me. Shit, I've been through so much with you, I had to forgive her. If I could make love to you after you gave birth to another man's baby then I for sure could make love to her after she lied about her identity. You've done far worse things to me."

Carmen narrowed her eyes as once again Kane threw light on the past. He had done it before, months ago, when they were headed to Georgia to deal with their daughter's kidnapping. He had called out all of her wrongdoings by name. She didn't respond to him then and she wasn't going to respond now. If anything, she wanted to end the conversation so she could focus on things which truly mattered like *Fresh Prince* and her wedding.

"I'm not going to go back and forth with you," Carmen told him. "If that's what you're looking for me to do, it's not going to happen. I want us to be cordial even if we can't be friends."

"You know I'll always love you."

"And I'll always love you." She expected her words to generate a response from Kane, but he only stared at her. Perhaps he was shocked she said the words back. It wasn't a secret she loved him; she simply wasn't *in love* with him. Or at least, she wasn't anymore.

His silence made Carmen turn towards her computer. She checked her emails as a sign to Kane the conversation was over. He obviously took the hint because he made his way towards the door. When he reached for the doorknob, she spoke. "Make sure you tell Monifah I said hello." They met eyes for a short moment yet her words didn't yield a response. He simply left the room. Once he did, his departure reminded her that Kristian was still in Georgia. She gave her strict orders to return home, but she hadn't heard anything from her. Not wanting to wait too late, Carmen picked up her phone and dialed Kristian's cell. As expected, her daughter didn't answer.

***

Kristian was still asleep on Victor's bare chest. Her cell phone, now in his hands, had been placed on silent hours earlier due to the large number of texts she received. Most of them Victor read upon receipt, learning she had recently broken up with a boy named Dijuan. In addition, a friend of hers named Coco sent her a long text telling her she was pregnant and marrying her brother, King, at the end of the year. It was soon followed by a text from her brother apologizing for Coco's pregnancy and explaining how he planned to be a good father and husband. Now, her mother had called her.

"I'm sorry if I scared you last night."

Victor looked down at his chest not knowing Kristian was awake. He quickly set her phone on the bedside dresser.

"The nightmares have been pretty frequent. No one knows about 'em, but my dad."

"You're fine," Victor whispered. He placed his fingers in her hair only to massage her scalp. Kristian closed her eyes at his touch. Both of them were completely silent until she sat up. She then got out of bed. "I guess you need to get home."

"I do," Kristian replied. She walked over to the bedside dresser and picked up her cell phone. She didn't have any unread messages until she checked her text message folder. It was then she saw texts not only from Dijuan and Coco, but also from King. According to the timestamp in her phone, each one was sent while she was asleep. Since the messages weren't marked, she knew Victor had read her texts. She went through each one learning her best friend was pregnant by her brother and planning to marry him on December 31st. Unsure of how to take the news or respond, Kristian turned her phone off. She didn't even bother to question Victor about the invasion of privacy. It was miniscule compared to the news that her best friend was pregnant by her brother.

Victor watched her until she went inside the bathroom. While she showered, he tried to come up with a way to make her stay. Unable to come up with a logical reason, he accepted she was leaving. He pushed the covers away from him, deciding to use the time to get dressed. Her mother was already on her trail and the last thing he wanted was for her to end up on his doorstep next.

Thankfully, he didn't have a run-in with her. By mid-afternoon, Kristian was back in Brookstone. He learned of her arrival in New York via text as did Carmen who received the message during an impromptu meeting at Flame. For the first ten minutes after receiving the news, Carmen debated about whether or not to leave work early. A part of her wanted to rush over to Kane's condo and confront her daughter while another part simply wanted to hold her in her arms. Certain the latter was going to happen, Carmen left work at her regular time.

Upon reaching her limo, she called Kane to make sure Kristian was home only to be told they were on their way to Manhattan. Apparently, his parents had been requesting for the two to visit more frequently. Now that Kristian had returned to Brookstone, he decided it was a good time to make the trip.

Since she wouldn't be seeing her daughter that night, she told Gully to head home. With so much on her mind—from her daughter, to Kane's surprise visit at Flame—Carmen was silent for most of the ride. She figured Gully caught wind of her mood because he didn't attempt at small talk. He pulled up to her house without them even having a conversation. However, once she went inside, her energy changed. She stood in the doorway to see Rakim and Nyla cruising around in Rakim's battery-powered Mercedes Benz while Jay watched from the bottom of the stairwell. She instantly got their attention as they got hers. She then became more vocal as if nothing was wrong.

It wasn't until hours later after the kids were in bed that she remembered the divorce papers. She and Jay were on their way to their room when the thought popped in her head. "Why don't we walk to the garden?"

Jay narrowed his eyes because it was rare he and Carmen ever ventured to that part of the estate. The garden was an area designed more for show than actual use. It also remained hidden since it was located behind the swimming pool and pool house. "We need privacy or something?"

"No, it's peaceful." Privacy never crossed Carmen's mind because she was certain there was a lack of it. Three men—Roman, Gully, and Linx—were around twenty-four seven so privacy was never expected. Her divorce wasn't a secret, anyway. Instead of waiting for a response, she headed down the steps to the home office. She had placed the papers there shortly after dinner. She grabbed the manila envelope from the desk and when she went in the foyer, she saw Jay at the back door waiting on her. They walked to the garden and once they were seated on a granite bench, she handed him the envelope. "Everything is done."

Jay opened the envelope, but didn't read much of the contents. There was no need in his opinion. Carmen was officially a single woman and while they wouldn't be married until next year, she was now all his. "This right here," he began, speaking slowly, "means everything."

"I know it does, which is why I wanted to tell you in person. I've had the papers since this morning. I could've told you over the phone, but I wanted you to see it."

Jay set the envelope in her lap. "I've waited a long time for this, you know?" A soft chuckle escaped his lips. "I feel like Jacob. I worked all these years to get one woman."

His words stung and even created an influx of past memories. Although guilt and blame fell on both their hands, Carmen knew she could write a laundry list of the hurt and pain she caused alone. "I wish you didn't have to feel that way. I wish I could've gotten it right the first time. But even that thought feels wrong. If I hadn't married Kane, I wouldn't have Kristian. I also wouldn't have Akaila and Malachi. It was Kane's idea to adopt them."

"I know what you mean," Jay mumbled. "I'm not offended." He looked around the garden as an awkward silence filled the air. To add to the mood, he suddenly remembered the secret he'd been withholding. With a fresh start on the horizon, it was the best time to come clean. "There's something I need to tell you." He met eyes with Carmen yet no other words came out his mouth.

"What is it?" Carmen asked, hearing the silence.

While he was getting ready to tell her the estate was Casa de Sangre, he began to have second thoughts. The estate, nicknamed the House of Blood, by his father's men, was the site of many brutal and violent "business" meetings. A large part of his life, he lived there since birth until he was a teenager. He left the property after his mother's suicide and moved into a new home purchased with his inheritance. He didn't hear of Carmen's interest in the estate until after she had ended their engagement. Hurt over the decision, to get back at her, he listed the home's owner as a business entity and upped the selling price. At the closing, he sent an old associate of his father's in his place as the company's face.

Since Carmen didn't know he owned the estate, she also didn't know part of his income came from the millions he received from the sale. She also didn't know she was sleeping in the very same room where his parents were murdered. Jay wasn't numb to his parents' deaths so he only pretended to be comfortable for the sake of Carmen and the kids. He also knew their stay there would be short-lived. Right after their wedding, he planned to break ground on a new estate, one bigger than what Carmen now owned. He planned to have the property finished by the time their first anniversary came around. This way, he could give Carmen something bigger and better as well as get away from Casa de Sangre.

"Jay?" Carmen said his name now slightly concern. He wasn't speaking despite telling her he wanted to share something with her. "What is it? Just tell me. I can handle it."

Jay knew the right thing to do was to tell her, but he couldn't find it in himself to do so. It would hurt her to know he swindled millions out of her because he wanted revenge. "I don't know why I said that, Peaches. Everything's cool."

"Are you sure?"

Jay placed a kiss on her lips to soothe her suspicions. "Yeah, it's nothing." He eased out a small smile, which seemed to do the trick. She dropped the subject all together as did he. With nothing left to discuss, Jay led the way inside. They retired to their bedroom, both of them heading in the bathroom to start their nightly routine. Shortly thereafter, they were in bed, lying in each other's arms. Carmen's eyes were closed, but Jay quickly learned she wasn't asleep.

"You know you can tell me anything, right?"

Jay didn't respond because he wasn't sure if he could. There were things he told her in the past, which almost ended their relationship. It was one of the reasons he was reluctant to tell her about Case de Sangre. "Well, you can," she continued. "You always can." Jay heard her loud and clear, but didn't believe her words. For that reason, he didn't speak. When he finally did, almost two hours later, Carmen was fast asleep.

"We'll see, Peaches," he whispered. "We'll see."

9

All Night

Jay was still awake four hours after his head hit the pillow. Thoughts of Casa de Sangre and his parents were still on his mind, making it hard for him to sleep. The couple of times he tried, his eyes naturally reopened. Once he realized he was fighting a losing battle, he decided to head downstairs. He could finish reading the article he'd found earlier, do more research on conflict diamonds, and finish off the Italian crème cake in the fridge. Then, once his eyes got heavy, he could get back in bed. A feasible plan, he pulled himself away from Carmen. She didn't stir so he grabbed the newspaper and headed downstairs. Halfway down the steps, he discovered Gully in the foyer. "You're still here?" Gully did a half-turn when he learned he had an audience. "I thought you went home after dinner."

"I went to the pool house," Gully replied. "Roman and I were playing chess."

Jay looked at him strangely because a chess game didn't explain why he was standing in his foyer in the middle of the night. "Your chess game is over. Get some sleep. Seven forty-five will be here before you know it."

"We take turns watching the estate at night," Gully explained.

Jay didn't wait for Gully to elaborate as he remembered why he was downstairs in the first place. Still carrying his newspaper, he headed towards the kitchen. He went inside, going straight to the fridge. Gully joined him and while his cousin didn't ask for any, he passed him a slice of cake on a saucer. They then walked to the home office. A room they once knew as the parlor, it was the place where his father would retire after dinner.

"A lot has changed in here," Gully noticed. "You didn't mind Carmen changing the décor? This was your father's man cave."

"That's a secret," Jay announced. "Don't mention that around Carmen."

"What's a secret? Carmen knows this is your house, right?"

"No, she doesn't," Jay clarified. "So like I said, keep your mouth closed." Jay flipped through the pages of *The Brookstone Times* until he got to the *World* section. "Besides, she owns this now."

"That's some bullshit. So you have your fiancée paying you thousands each month while you rest your head next to her. She should be living here scot free." Gully shook his head at how conning his cousin could be. "How do you even have sex in that room?"

Jay was taken aback. As a result, his eyes became watery and itchy almost as if he was becoming allergic to something in the air. Gully's question was too sensitive to answer. Unsure of what to say, he felt a sense of relief when he heard footsteps on the stairwell. Seconds later, Carmen appeared in the doorway.

"You couldn't sleep?" she asked.

Jay looked at Gully, but his cousin didn't even look in his direction. He simply said excuse me and left the room. "I couldn't. Did I wake you?"

Carmen walked further in the office. "No, I had to use the bathroom. When I saw you weren't in bed, I went looking for you. You weren't in the kids' rooms so I checked down here." Carmen walked around the desk until she was standing beside him. "So are you looking up things for the wedding? Or are you trying to sneak and buy your Christmas gifts?"

"A little bit of both," Jay lied. He slid his chair back so Carmen could sit in his lap. He knew she was being nosy when she picked up the newspaper. "Regular old news," he told her.

"I see." Carmen's eyes traveled over the desk yet the only thing she noticed was the Italian crème cake. "So you can't sleep and you're hungry. That's a bad combination."

"And I'm trying to buy your Christmas gifts, not to mention, plan our honeymoon," Jay lied.

Jay watched as Carmen got up from his lap. He wanted her to leave, but he didn't expect her to be so abrupt. "I'll be up soon," he told her when he realized she was leaving. "You don't have to wait up." She stopped in the doorway to face him.

"I won't," she replied. "You have the room all to yourself. Spend as much money as you like on me. Oh, and for the honeymoon, pick a place that has a beach and a lot of sun."

Jay cracked a smile as she closed the door. *Whatever you want, Peaches.* He chuckled at the thought as he looked at the newspaper. He started to read the article, forgetting about the lies he told. Not once did he look up anything regarding their honeymoon or Christmas. It was as if the more he read about conflict diamonds, the more he wanted to know. The scandal was his main focus until his eyes grew heavy. Once he could no longer keep his eyes opened, he retired to his bedroom.

10

Four Door Aventador
Christmas

An unexpected breeze swept over Carmen's face, causing her to stir. Well aware it was Christmas morning, her eyes naturally opened. She looked to the right of her only to see Jay wasn't there. When she felt even more of a wind chill, she assumed he was on the balcony. It was an odd place for him to be since the balcony still contained remnants of a recent blizzard. The area rarely got sunlight so the snow and ice were taking longer to melt. To Carmen, it was a danger zone.

If he needed privacy, he could've gone to a guest room. Why stand in the freakin' cold?

Carmen climbed out of bed to see where he was. She walked to the balcony to see him standing there, fully clothed, with a rarely worn pair of work boots on his feet. His cell phone was also to his ear. His lips moved rapidly as if he was trying to squeeze a twenty minute call into five seconds. Unsure of who he was speaking to, she instantly became suspicious.

For the past couple of weeks, she had watched him spend most of his evenings and nights in the home office. He would joke and say he was finishing up his Christmas shopping, but none of the presents under the tree were from him. It made her wonder if he had gotten anyone anything. He tried to use their wedding as an excuse, but he missed the second meeting they had with their wedding planners.

"I need to make sure of some things," he was saying. "I need to know what I'm dealing with." Unbeknownst to Carmen, a loud sigh emerged on the other end of the call. The exhalation was made by Grendel, a man she had never met. She continued to watch Jay even when he learned of her presence. "I have to go. We'll talk later."

Carmen swallowed as Jay hung up the phone. She knew he stopped speaking because of her. From hearing the tail-end of the conversation, she knew the call had zero to do with Christmas. Something else was brewing, which made her put the words, *mysterious phone call,* on the blackboard of her mind. She wore her suspicions on her face so she quickly changed expressions. She gave him a broad smile and though it was returned, it wasn't genuine.

Despite being caught, Jay remained in character. He opened one of the French doors, allowing more cold air to fill the room. "Nosy ass," he joked. "Can I at least get one of your gifts here without you knowing?"

Carmen's smile didn't fade although she was being lied to. "It should already be here," she argued, playfully. "Your gift is here. I got it here despite the snow. You should've started your shopping in September. That way, you wouldn't have to stand in the freezing cold to take a call."

"It's not even that cold out there," Jay differed. "Besides, I was talking to a contractor I was thinking of using for the wedding."

Little did Jay know, Carmen saw through the whole conversation. He couldn't have been speaking with a contractor for the wedding when he hadn't attended any meetings. Instead of calling him out, she played along. "Don't worry about it today," she told him. "We still have a year."

A small smile emerged on Jay's face until his mind went to his call with Grendel. He had reached out to him, detailing everything he'd learned. Grendel was impressed at his knowledge, but there was still more to be gathered. The only way to truly know if he was playing a role in the scandal was to put a closer set of eyes on his African comrade. The only question was when.

"Something is bothering you," Carmen voiced. She studied Jay's face, seeing a mix of disappointment and concern. "I can see it. You got wrinkles on your forehead; your mouth is turned upside down. Is it the wedding? You still haven't told me why you missed another meeting. Do you know I started working on the guest list? We also looked at different designs for the Save the Date."

Jay knew she was concerned, but at times, he wished she simply didn't ask. Her questions would only make him lie to her again.

"You're being tightlipped," Carmen muttered. "You did this to me before. Remember when we were in the garden and you wanted to tell me something? You were about to and then all of a sudden you changed your mind."

Jay closed his eyes as she reminded him of the secret he was withholding. The conversation had gone from one extreme to the next. "Look, let's just…" Jay was caught off guard when he heard Rakim in the hallway. Now learning he was awake, he listened as he tried to open the baby gate. "He saw the Hummer," he explained, bolting towards the bedroom door.

"The Hummer?" Carmen questioned. She remained in place only because she wasn't appropriately dressed. "There's a Hummer under the Christmas tree?"

"Yeah, I got it to go with his Benz. Roman brought it over for me. I hid my gifts at Blue Magic." Jay opened the door, allowing Rakim's screams of excitement to fill the room. "Let me get him before he jumps over the gate. I can hear him trying to break it open. We'll finish this later."

Carmen took a deep breath because she knew later wasn't going to come. Jay wanted to dodge the conversation all together. When she heard the roar of Rakim's Hummer from downstairs, she decided to let the issue go. Jay would be her husband in exactly a year and she had to trust he was making the right decisions for their family. If she didn't, their relationship would fail.

With a new outlook on the day, Carmen headed to the bathroom so she could shower and dress. By the time she made it downstairs, the foyer was full of wrapping paper and opened presents. In addition, Gully, King, and Malachi were now at the house. Carmen didn't yet open her gifts, choosing to clean up the foyer a bit. When Jay saw what she was doing, he interrupted her.

"Were you looking for this?"

Carmen looked at him to see him holding a portrait. "What's that?"

Jay didn't answer her question. "Can you clear some space on the table?"

They were standing in front of the dining room so instead of probing him more, Carmen did as he asked. Once the space was clear, Jay set the frame on the table and told her the gift was all hers. Carmen took her time opening it, studying the shape and size as she guessed what it could be. Certain he wouldn't choose something obvious, she tried to think outside the box. Not a single idea came to mind. When she did finally peel off the wrapping paper, the first thing she noticed was the gold frame. Then, as more of the picture became visible, she realized it wasn't a portrait per se. It was a multi-level floor plan.

"Our relationship, our marriage, is all about building a home," Jay began, "but I also want to build a house. I want something from scratch."

"Wow," Carmen mouthed. "I'm actually speechless on this one."

"I knew you would be." Jay started to say more until he was interrupted by the doorbell. He looked in the foyer and when he saw King headed for the front door, he continued speaking. "No one knows about this, but you. I don't want to say anything until we break ground."

Carmen ran her fingers along the glass as if she could feel the ink from the blueprint. "I love this. Well, now that I know what I'm looking at," she clarified. "It's just that..." she paused, "...I've spent millions on this property. This place was on the market for a long time before I bought it.

What if it doesn't sell?" Carmen took her hands off the portrait. She had doubts, but she didn't want Jay to think she wasn't appreciative.

"Sell, rent, lease, whatever we do, I promise you'll make your money back. Let that be my concern. In the meantime, where's my Christmas gift?"

Carmen grinned only because she wasn't quite sure if he was ready for his present. She had gone all out or so she thought until she saw what he got her. What she bought him was expensive, but it didn't top a mansion. "I guess you can have it now. You deserve it." She followed her reply with a kiss, which was cut short when she heard three new voices in the house. She looked in the foyer to see Kristian, Kane, and Monifah. She assumed her and her ex would be spending the holidays apart, but it was obvious he received an invitation to the festivities.

"You didn't tell me he was coming," Jay whispered, harshly.

"I didn't know he was coming. I thought Kristian was coming by herself." Carmen watched as Kristian went to the Christmas tree looking for her gifts. Kane and Monifah remained in place as if they didn't know what to do. "Let's just say hi," Carmen suggested. "I'll give Kane his gift, and he can be on his way."

"I don't even want to do that."

Carmen ignored his statement as she walked to the foyer. When she entered, she noticed Akaila coming down the steps. Carmen approached Kane and Monifah while Akaila headed to the Christmas tree. "Happy Holidays," Carmen greeted. She eyed Monifah purposely. "I didn't know y'all were coming."

"It was sort of last minute," Monifah replied. She played along to Carmen's fakeness although she knew her presence wasn't welcomed. "When we were opening gifts at home, Kristian mentioned having to come over here. We figured we could at least show our faces. We won't stay for dinner. I cooked a meal so we could take a plate over to Sanders." Monifah spoke of Kane's old partner who had been paralyzed by Blu's men. He currently resided in a rehab facility as he adjusted to his new life. "We also have an announcement to make."

"Is that right?" Carmen narrowed her eyes until she felt Jay's frame hovering over her. When his arms wrapped around her waist, her face softened. She could hear him telling her to remain cool although he hadn't spoken a single word. She looked at Monifah waiting for her to deliver the news, but it was actually Kane who spoke.

"Monifah and I got married."

Carmen listened as the entire room fell silent. She wasn't shocked at the news, already suspecting it when Monifah used the word, "announcement." She simply didn't know what to say.

"No one is going to say congratulations?" Kane looked at every face in the room. From what he could see, everyone was wearing a blank stare.

"Congratulations," Akaila blurted, her face void of a smile.

Her sarcasm changed the room's vibe from bad to worse. It then took another turn when Kristian stood up, grabbed what presents she could, and headed upstairs. Akaila followed behind her, later joined by Malachi. The only children with Kane's last name, Carmen realized they were taking it harder than anyone else. Even King didn't look upset, just a little taken aback.

"Maybe one day, everyone can accept it," Kane proposed.

"Who said we didn't?" King snapped. "We're shocked not upset."

Carmen started to soften the mood until Jay whispered in her ear. He was ready for his gift and considering the tension, it was probably best for them to make an exit. Separating herself from him, she headed to the Christmas tree where she picked up a small, red box. She then went to the home office to grab her keys.

"We're going outside?" Jay questioned once she was at the front door.

"Yep, you know it's not too cold." Carmen gave him a crooked smile as she reminded him of his phone call.

Jay overlooked the comment to keep from revisiting the topic. To further distract her, he opened the door and walked outside. She was right on his heel so he made small talk about all the random places everyone hid their gifts to keep her from mentioning the phone call.

"I put your gift in the garage because I knew it was a place you wouldn't look," Carmen told him. She pressed a button on the remote key to open the garage door. "None of the limousines are parked there. What reason do you have to go inside? I mean, it's not like you work on cars."

Jay chuckled. "True. You picked a good spot." Jay took a step closer to the garage as the door slowly started to rise. The anticipation was killing him and his eyes naturally widened as he took note of a small automobile inside. A black car cover hung tightly over the vehicle, accentuating the frame of the sports car. "Did you really do this?" Jay walked away from the garage in disbelief. "That can't be what I think it is."

Carmen laughed loudly at Jay's reaction. He continuously paced the driveway although he hadn't seen the car in its true glory. Since the garage door was fully raised, Carmen stepped inside and grabbed the car cover. "Want to help me do the honors?"

"You are out of your fuckin' mind. I want to see your checkbook. Ain't no way—"

"Hey, my gift doesn't *even* compare to what you're spending on our new house," Carmen shot back. "Now, shut up, and accept the gift. Besides, you'll have the title."

Jay shook his head as he walked inside the garage. Ready to unveil his new sports car, he reached down and grabbed the car cover. He pulled it off the car, saying, "You know they took my license."

"You'll get it back when they drop your charges. That's the reason why I got this for you. I wanted you to have something to look forward to."

Jay grinned at her response as a Lamborghini Aventador was displayed. The Superveloce model was painted a glittered red. Ready to get the car on the road, he watched as Carmen dangled a box in front of him. "You're crazy for this, you know that?" He pulled the box from her hands and worked double time taking the wrapping paper off. "You went all out on this one. I still can't believe this."

"Believe it," Carmen replied. She walked to the passenger side and waited. She knew Jay wanted to take the car for a spin and with the kids chaperoned, there wasn't much stopping him.

When he got inside, he didn't immediately put the key in the ignition. Instead, he took his time examining the interior. He ran his fingertips along the carbon fiber dashboard, leather seats, and even the door handles. He then opened each compartment he could find before peeling off the steering wheel cover. When he did finally start the car, he sat there for a minute or two, listening to the soft roar of the engine. "I want to move this so bad," he expressed. "I can't risk it, though."

"You don't have that much longer to wait." Carmen rested her hand upon his, interlocking their fingers together. His skin was rough against hers, the callus feel awakening dead memories. Rewind twenty or so odd years, she remembered meeting him in a diner in West Brookstone. One peek in his direction and he caught her eye. Ruggedly handsome and nearly bald, everything about him intrigued her. From the way his strides exuded power to his extreme rawness, his hardcore persona opened her up to a brand new world.

"Did I tell you I took King to the diner where we met? We ate in the exact booth you and Tiara were in."

"That's funny," Carmen said. "I was just thinking of that." Carmen's eyes widened at how peculiar it was for them to be sharing the same thought.

"Out of all the places we could've gone that day, Tiara had to choose that diner. She knew I wasn't comfortable being on the Westside. She dragged me there and the unforgettable happened."

"I was embarrassed when you caught me staring at you."

Carmen chuckled loudly as she remembered the way he acted. "Carlos told everyone you were staring at me." The memory tickled her even more as she recalled how Jay pretended to be eating his food when his friend called him out. "So what were you thinking when you saw me?"

"You mean aside from my mind being in the gutter?" Jay laughed when he saw a flash of annoyance appear in Carmen's eyes. "No, I just knew something about you was different. I couldn't put my finger on it. Then, I was nervous because I didn't think you would go for a guy like me. I was so reckless. I couldn't let my demons stop me from being with you, though."

Carmen tightened her grip around his fingers. "I'm glad you didn't."

An uncomfortable stretch of silence appeared as they met eyes. Unsure of what each other was thinking; the gaze was broken when Jay turned away. "Why do you want to marry me? When I look back, I put you through a lot. There was that fight at your parents' house where I almost pushed you down the stairs, the time I said I was messing with my ex, when I wasn't, just to hurt you. Then, the worst of it all, the morning I almost killed you. I almost killed King."

Carmen closed her eyes as he brought up the most tumultuous time of their relationship. During the early days of the Santiago cartel, she secretly worked for him under the tutelage of his best friend, Carlos. In an effort to get money to fund Flame, she agreed to steal a briefcase of diamonds to sell at a Diamond Exchange conference, not knowing the diamonds belonged to Jay. To add to the madness, in exchange for Carlos' silence, she committed the ultimate act of betrayal. When Jay discovered her infidelity and thieving ways, he unleashed violently, killing Carlos, and sending her on her back to Brookstone General Hospital. It was there she learned she was two months' pregnant with King.

"I forgave you for all that," she told him. "We grew from it, we healed, and we put it behind us. Besides, I played a role in some of that, too." Carmen raised his hand to her lips and kissed it. "We don't need to dig into the past. We're not those people anymore. That's the reason I'm marrying you. Regardless of the situation, you overcame every opposition, every obstacle. Anything anyone threw at you, you dealt with it and you handled it. You showed me you could be a better man." Carmen kissed his hand again. "I," she went on, "actually have another gift for you."

"Does it involve a three-letter word?"

Carmen's lips curled into a smile. "In a way," she stressed. She neared her head to his and gave him a small peck on the lips. "I took a pregnancy test a couple of days ago. It came back positive." Her lips, still curled in the smile, grew larger as her secret was out. It didn't fade until she noticed the blank expression Jay was giving her. In fact, he was showing very little emotion.

For Jay, at that moment, the half million dollar car, Casa de Sangre, the diamond scandal, all of it became miniscule. What now mattered was the woman in front of him who was carrying another seed that would carry the Santiago name. Within a matter of seconds, his excitement became displayed. From the warm whispers he slid in her ear to the soft caresses he gave her lower stomach, everything about his mood let Carmen know he was happy. Nevertheless, it all changed when he heard Kane and Monifah in the front yard. From what Jay could hear, they were scoping out the sports car. The moment was now lost. Neither he nor Carmen spoke until Kane and Monifah were gone. Once their audience had left, they resumed their conversation and even made a decision to keep the pregnancy a secret until after the first trimester.

Despite the news never leaving his lips, the topic remained on Jay's mind. Potential baby names constantly floated around in his head and he even got the idea of them moving briefly to San Juan so Carmen could give birth there. Thoughts he planned on sharing, he never got the chance. Hours later, when they finally settled in bed, Jay thought to bring the topic up until he noticed Carmen was asleep in his arms. Well aware the day had been tiresome, he didn't wake her. With months to prepare, there was plenty of time to plan and converse. For now, they could simply rest in the moment.

11

Buy a Heart

In Jay's opinion, the pregnancy was easy to keep under wraps. On Christmas, most of the talk around the house was centered on Kane's surprise marriage. A few days later, everyone's focus was Victor's criminal trial, which concluded with a not guilty verdict. Now, with New Year's Eve upon them, the attention shifted to King and Coco. The day of the wedding, Jay stood in one of the classrooms at Carmen's church, helping Malachi get ready. He locked an emerald cufflink on his shirt cuff while Carmen straightened his bowtie.

"You have the ring?" he heard Carmen ask.

"It's in my pocket," Malachi replied. He tapped the area so she would know something was there. "King gave it to me this morning. He told me if I lost it, I lost my life."

Carmen giggled at the threat. "Well, so far, so good, right? You're still in one piece." She finished with his bowtie just as King and Nicholas walked in the room. The door was still ajar so Tiara slid inside asking for help with Coco's dress. With only twenty minutes until the ceremony, Carmen quickly obliged.

With Carmen out the room, Jay decided it was the perfect time to have a conversation with King. He pulled him to the side and asked him to take a walk. They left the room, ending up in a small walkway between the church and resource center. Jay didn't speak right off, first grabbing his son's bowtie, pretending to straighten it, although it was already perfect. "One thing I could never teach you is how to be a husband. I've never been one. But, I can tell you the kind of husband I want to be." Jay pulled his hands from his son's neck and draped his arms at his side. "Then again, I much rather show you."

"I see how you treat my mom."

Jay cracked a smile. "Keep God first," he told him, not addressing his statement. "God comes before your wife. If you work on becoming a better man for God then you can be a better man for her. Then, you can be a better man for your children. That's what I'm working on now. I say we take the trek together."

King appreciated his father's words as evident by their embrace. Way shorter than Jay, clocking in at only 5'9", his head naturally hit his father's shoulder. "So, I have to get married for you to say all that?" He pulled away, allowing Jay to see the grin plastered on his face. "I'm kidding. I know how you feel. See…" King stuttered over his words when he saw Gully approaching. His cousin appeared uneasy as if he was coming to deliver bad news. Instantly thinking the worst, he remained quiet as Gully whispered a few words in Jay's ear.

"There's a man in the courtyard asking for you. He looks like one of us."

One of us only meant one thing in Jay's book. The man was Puerto Rican. Well aware of the man's identity, he cut his conversation with King short. "You better get inside. The ceremony is going to be starting soon." Jay didn't give King a chance to respond. He immediately walked away, Gully following in his footsteps, as he continued their conversation. "I need you to grab Linx for me. Tell him to meet me in the courtyard."

"Who is this guy?" Gully asked. "He's built like a fuckin' ox."

"He's an old friend. Can you get Linx?"

"I'll get him. Are you sure you want to meet this guy?"

"I got this," Jay replied as he took off for the courtyard. He heard Gully mumble something under his breath, but he didn't ask what he said. It was pointless anyway because his cousin was headed back in the church. Before long, Linx was catching up to him.

"You're bringing business to King's wedding?" Linx asked.

Jay looked at him to see an expression similar to Gully's. Both of them were thinking the worst.

"I'm holding," Linx disclosed. "Are you holding? Shit, you're always holding."

Jay wore a smile inside though one wasn't on his face. Both his cousin and right-hand were overly concerned about nothing. If they really knew him, like he thought they did, they would've known the last place he would bring any corrupt business was to his son's wedding. If anything, he doubled up on security so the event would go off without a hitch.

"Tell me what's going on." Linx pressed him for details.

"How about stand here and don't move." Jay stopped walking as the entrance to the courtyard was only a few feet away. While his visitor's presence couldn't be seen, they only needed to take a few more steps before he would become visible. "I'm serious, Linx. Don't say anything, just stand here."

"Who is this?"

Jay didn't bother to answer as he made his way into the courtyard. As expected, Linx followed behind him, but stopped at the entrance. Or so he thought. When he felt him brush past him, he grabbed his arm and pulled him violently behind him. He held him in place, knowing he had spotted Cesar. Another right-hand of his, Jay faked his death months ago to keep him from being implicated in the shooting at Blue Magic. So far, the plan was working well. Cesar moved to Canada and commuted between there and New York for work. He currently led a new security team hired by Jay to protect his family. The group, who Jay referred to as his ghosts, consisted of several men, all handpicked by Cesar, who was certified TTG—trained to go. They moved around the city like regular civilians and served as back-up for Gully, Roman, and Linx.

A top secret group, no one knew they existed. Although Jay was allowing Linx to see Cesar, he still would know nothing about his ghosts. The only reason Linx was in the courtyard was so that he would know Cesar was still alive. The two had natural chemistry from the days they spent running the streets of San Juan to their transition to the states to work for him. While Linx's surprise reaction was expected, Jay needed him to remain calm. "Don't draw too much attention," he pressed. "Kane is around here somewhere and who knows what members of the Triad are lurking. They know I have a trial coming up. They'll pin whatever they can on me. Just stand at the entrance and keep watch."

Jay could feel hesitation on Linx's part, which is why he didn't immediately let go of him. It wasn't until he felt a sense of composure that he released his grip and headed towards Cesar. A quick handshake was exchanged before Jay got down to business. "I got an assignment for you."

"You know my team can handle it," Cesar replied with a grin. "Lay it on me."

Jay shook his head as he reached inside his black tuxedo jacket. He pulled out a small stack of folded papers, which he handed over. "I don't need your team. It's a solo mission. It's one I wanted to take, but with King's wedding and the trial coming up, I can't get away. Those documents tell you exactly where you need to go."

Despite having the papers in his hand, Cesar didn't unfold them. Instead, he eyed Jay carefully, hoping he would say more. When the glare didn't prompt a response, he opened the papers and started to read. At the first sentence, he almost handed the documents back to him. "You're sending me to Kenema? Who are you gunning after in Africa?"

"No one," Jay answered, sharply. "Yet."

Cesar took a second glance at the papers, continuing to read. "That's it? You just want me to find this man in the picture and watch him?"

"That's all," Jay confirmed. "More than likely, he already knows who you are. I suggest you keep yourself as invisible as possible."

Cesar nodded his head in agreement although he wasn't exactly sure what he was getting himself into. The good part about the assignment was that he didn't have to talk to anyone. He only needed to keep an eye out for one particular person. "I'm in, but can we discuss flights, car service, what about a hotel—"

"Page three and four," Jay replied, turning on his heel. "I got you." He walked forward, facing Linx, knowing they needed to get inside. "I gotta go," he said, loud enough for Cesar to hear. "You know how to reach me." He tapped Linx's shoulder as he passed him as a way to tell him to follow suit.

"Ser buen, hermano."

Linx's words, "Be good, brother," caught Jay off guard yet it didn't stop him from making his way to the church. Although he felt he owed Linx more time with Cesar, he had to make sure they stayed protected. It was one of the reasons he handpicked Cesar to go to Africa. If anyone did see him at the wedding, he would be out the country before they could find him.

"Where were you?" Carmen yelled, appearing out of nowhere. She was slightly out of breath, which told Jay she had been searching for him. "Did you forget your son is getting married?"

Carmen's tone was ferocious, but Jay didn't fire back. He simply stared at her as she turned around and headed towards the church. He didn't think his conversation with Cesar lasted long, but Carmen made it seem like he had delayed the wedding. When he walked in the church's foyer, he learned the ceremony was not yet underway. The stage was empty with the exception of the band who was set up to the far left, currently playing a soft rendition of a ballad. Jay listened as Carmen barked orders at whoever she could. Then, she started in on him.

"I left to help Coco and you did a disappearing act. This better not happen at our wedding."

Jay cracked a smile at Carmen's small tantrum. He knew he hadn't truly upset her. She was simply nervous about King getting married and taking it out on him. He became certain of it when their minister approached the stage. At the sight of Bro. Harrison, Carmen grabbed his hand, intertwining their fingers together. Her grip tightened when King took the stage. His groomsmen then followed suit.

While Jay remained relaxed, a slight breath escaped Carmen's lips. Her son was in front of her, standing at the altar, but she also saw him sitting in a therapist's office as a troubled seven year-old boy. The vision was only the beginning of more intense memories. From her days of packing his belongings to send him to a treatment facility to the numerous times she visited him in a detention center. Despite his disturbing beginnings, the latter years of his life became promising. An accomplishment he didn't make by himself, Carmen had to give credit to Jay. By allowing King to play a role in his businesses, the hot-tempered son she once knew had vanished.

"We're about to get started," an usher announced.

Carmen's attention went back to the happenings in the foyer. Maya was now in front of her, the first in the processional, while Kane and Monifah stood behind her and Jay. An idea of King's to show his admiration and respect for his stepfather, it was a detail of the wedding Jay never spoke of. All eyes were officially on them as the band's lead vocalist sung the opening notes of Ed Sheeran's "Thinking Out Loud." Already nervous, the singer's soulful tone made Carmen succumb even more to her feelings. She walked down the aisle, studying her son's face, as tears fell down her own.

King's smile radiated through the room like sunlight beaming through stained glass windows. An indescribable peace surrounded him, fluttering Carmen's heart and picking at her emotions. Her eyes remained locked on him as her mind drifted again down memory lane. Vivid in her mind just like the present moment, Carmen cried harder. No longer her angel with broken wings, she listened as her firstborn said, "I do."

12

Anaconda

Only days since his son tied the knot, thoughts of King's wedding were already fleeting from Jay's mind. Slightly past eight o'clock, he waited behind a long line of cars on the Arrivals level of JFK International Airport. He was seated inside his Aventador as he clocked every area of Terminal 4 for a glimpse of Cesar. He hadn't spoken to his right-hand since King's wedding, their only communication being an email he received in which Cesar informed him he was about to board a plane to the states. Well aware Cesar could be bringing back sensitive information, he made it a point to drive alone.

He thought it was going to be hard to get away from the house, but he was mistaken. Once Gully and Roman started in on a game of chess, they forgot all about him. Linx, on the other hand, took the evening off to spend with his family. As for Carmen, she didn't question a thing when he told her he was heading to Blue Magic to do inventory. She easily bought the story. Now, he was at the airport waiting for Cesar to arrive. A total of ten minutes passed before his right-hand finally emerged through the airport's sliding doors. Once he took notice of Cesar, Jay honked his horn to get his attention. Cesar didn't see him at first so he honked again. This time, Cesar looked in his direction. Automatically, Cesar's mouth turned upside down.

"You shouldn't be doing this," were the first words out his mouth once he was inside the car. "You got three men who can drive you and you're risking your freedom like this?"

"Who else was going to scoop you?"

"I have a team, Jay. You pay 'em, I lead 'em. Remember?"

Jay cracked a smile, but wasn't quick to respond as he looked for a way out. A taxi was on his left so he waited for the vehicle to move before he took his foot off the brake. "Forget all that. Tell me what you saw. What kind of trouble am I looking at?" Jay glanced at Cesar and a part of him wished he hadn't. Cesar's face wore a look of immense concern and even a hint of fear. "Don't stall. I know it's bad. I can tell from the way you're looking at me."

"Kenema has been taken over by a brand new militia. They shut down the entire city council. That man you asked me to watch, I only saw him once the whole time I was there. He stays hidden and lives in a house your ass could only dream of owning. When I did see him, he was in a vehicle with about eight to ten assault rifles around him. Most of my information came from eavesdropping on civilian conversation. Rumor around town is that he's fighting to take over all of Sierra Leone."

Jay bit his bottom lip. "What about Kenema's mayor? What about the country's president?"

"The mayor is dead and his family, too. They were murdered by the militia so they could take over." Cesar paused as Jay drove away from the airport. "I went through crazy shit to get inside this city. I didn't know why until I saw what was going on. Praise God everything checked out."

Jay wiped his face as he learned he was in deeper than he thought. Grendel hadn't prepared him for what he was hearing. While he thought his African comrade was only a businessman who might have gotten caught up in a situation, it was the exact opposite. His African comrade *was* the situation. "Mayor is dead, president is dead. No one is there to stop him?"

"The president of Sierra Leone isn't dead. The president is the one fighting against the army to try and regain control of Kenema. He's losing men fast, though. He needs someone to intervene."

"I think America is trying, Amnesty, too," Jay admitted.

"Who?" Cesar asked not recognizing the name. Jay was set to explain, but his right-hand didn't give him a chance. "Don't worry about it, just tell me, is this what you wanted? I mean, did you suspect this was going on? Is that why you asked me to watch him?"

"I knew a war was going on," Jay confessed. "I thought my partner was caught up in it somehow, but I didn't think he was leading it. Now that I know he is, our partnership is over."

Cesar set further in his seat as a new idea entered his mind. "When Blu kidnapped Kristian, he kidnapped her in order to get something from you. He even had his men try and steal it. It's the reason you sent me to Florida. You wanted me to pick up a package. From what I recall, Blu wanted something in that package. Were there diamonds in there? Are you getting diamonds from this man in Africa?"

Jay dodged the question. "Those details aren't important anymore."

"What reason do you have to hold out on me?"

"Sometimes," Jay began, "lack of knowledge is a good thing."

Cesar grunted out of frustration. "Okay, Jay, keep your secrets, but if you fuck up, please believe, you'll need more than a team of men to keep your family from ending up like the mayor's."

A sour taste formed in Jay's mouth, a result of his uneasiness. He didn't want to admit he was fearful, yet he was. For once in his life, he felt he had finally met his match. His African comrade had an army while all he had was a bunch of bodyguards. He could never go up against him. Blu, on the other hand, was different. He was more of a thorn in his side while his business partner was a militant Mr. Untouchable. He told Grendel he would call him back with an answer and now he had to tell him he was bowing out. Their next conversation would be their last.

"How was King's wedding?"

Jay appreciated the sudden change in topics. "It was beautiful. We put together a lot in a short amount of time. In a way, helping him with his wedding was like practice for my own."

"Hopefully, with these huge steps he's taking, your relationship with him can get better. Marriage isn't easy. Fatherhood isn't either. If he isn't scared now, God knows he'll be once the baby comes."

Jay tightened his grip on the steering wheel. Two words in particular, scared, and God, resonated with him. He attributed his feelings towards his business partner until he recalled a past conversation with his mother.

Soft footsteps sounded in the hallway eventually stopping at his door. Jay figured it was his mother listening to see if he was up. Certain she would come inside, he continued reading until his door opened.

"What is it tonight, mijo?"

His mother spoke just above a whisper yet her strong Puerto Rican accent was still present. She didn't remain in the doorway long although he replied with, "Nothing." She quickly moved to the head of his bed where she took a seat, now in his body space. Jay closed the book he was reading. He set it on his bedside dresser only for his mother to pick it up. She flipped through the pages until she reached the page he bookmarked.

"The Great Gatsby," she exclaimed, reading the title. "Wow, Jay, you've gotten far in this. I hope you're doing the same in your bible studies. Did you read a scripture tonight?"

"Of course," Jay lied. He added on a smile, hoping she wouldn't press him for details. Nevertheless, he knew his mother. As expected, she asked him which one and he confidently replied with Psalms 27.

"Recite it," she ordered. She tapped his chest as an extra push. "Come on, let's hear it."

Certain it didn't begin with The Lord is my shepherd, I shall not want, Jay remained quiet. His silence lasted long enough for his mother to know he was fibbing. She didn't fuss at him for lying, but quickly quoted the chapter's first verse. She did it first in Spanish before repeating the words in English.

"The Lord is my light and my salvation whom shall I fear? The Lord is the stronghold of my life of whom shall I be afraid?"

His mother's voice echoed loudly in his ears as if she was right there next to him. Even though she wasn't, the thought of her being close calmed him. He loosened his grip on the steering wheel as he changed his mind about helping Grendel. It's like the scripture gave him the encouragement he needed. *I can't fear any man*, Jay thought. *Fear is only relative.*

"No fear," Jay stated, finally responding to Cesar. "Remember that."

***

Days since his encounter with Cesar, Jay hadn't yet made contact with Grendel. His hands were full dealing with the final touches on Iceland amongst the normal day to day operations of his other businesses. If he hadn't forced himself to stop working, he would've never gotten around to working on his honeymoon. Carmen had given him the responsibility of handling the details, and finding the perfect luxury houseboat was at the top of the list. His plan was for them to sail away after the reception to enjoy a night on the water, followed by a week-long stay on a Caribbean island. So far, he hadn't done much to make it happen so viewing a selection of boats made him feel as if he was making headway.

"How much did the guy say this was going for?"

Jay stepped in the boat's salon, hearing Gully behind him. He had brought his cousin along to be his voice of reason in the event he couldn't decide between some of the models. "Eight hundred thousand," Jay responded. He sat on a long, royal blue couch and stretched his legs out. "This one has four bedrooms. There's a laundry room, too."

"You'll need more than that if you ever use it for the family."

Jay agreed with him as he gave the salon the once-over. He was highly impressed, but he quickly reminded himself it was the first boat he'd seen. There were more expensive ones on the lot, which meant more rooms and better layouts.

"Does Carmen know about your plans?"

"Carmen doesn't even know I'm here," Jay replied with a chuckle. "She probably thinks I'm at Iceland." He stood on his feet only to feel his cell phone vibrating in his pants' pocket. "One second," he mumbled after reading Grendel's name on the home screen. He headed for the deck since the area appeared vacant. "Grendel," he greeted. "I was going to call you this week."

"I didn't know if you were or not. You're a busy man, Mr. Santiago. Your jewelry store is about to open, right?"

Jay smiled because it was obvious Grendel was keeping up with him. "It is. I hope to see you at the grand opening. I'll go ahead and tell you I found out a lot within the last couple of days. You were right. I am tied to something. This hits closer to home than I thought." Jay studied his surroundings to make sure he didn't have an audience. Although he didn't see anyone, he still chose his words carefully. "Do you know how much information the government has on this war?"

"They know almost everything."

"I figured that," Jay responded. He gazed at his surroundings again, not seeing anyone in earshot. "My business partner is over it, Grendel. I've received confirmation of that. He now controls the city. I've been supporting his cause not knowing where my money was going."

"I was hoping I wouldn't hear that," Grendel mumbled. "The government was simply operating off a hunch. No one had any actual evidence against you."

Jay heard disappointment in Grendel's voice, but he expected the opposite. Grendel came to him for a favor, which was to find out who was behind the blood diamonds scandal in Africa. "I think you forgot you wanted this. In order for me to help, I had to be involved. I haven't officially ceased my business relationship with him, but I'm going to. My advice is that you go ahead and give your connect at the White House the heads up. They have a fierce battle on their hands."

A long sigh, similar to the one Grendel had given him before, sounded. "Now that we know you two are indeed connected, are you willing to work with the White House to take him down? If you say yes, I promise, they'll forget about the Pink Sunrise."

Jay bit his lip as he recalled the code of the street. Snitching was more than frowned upon and also brought retaliation. If he testified against his partner, he was setting his family up as potential targets. That's if word ever got to his partner that he snitched. "Tell me something, Grendel, how are you going to protect me and my family?"

"Witness Protection will always be available."

"I'm not about to uproot my family's lives for this. Witness Protection? You have to come with something better." Automatically, Grendel started a verbal tirade. In the midst of it, Jay received an incoming call from Carmen. He ignored it, sending her to voicemail, only for her to call again. He didn't answer as he continued to listen to Grendel talk about the lives that had been lost at the hands of his partner. "I know what he's doing," Jay reminded him. "I'm well versed on what's going on, but who's going to protect my family if he finds out I was the one who ratted him out?"

"Mr. Santiago, I told you, Witness Protection."

Jay sucked his teeth. "Y'all motherfuckers are using me. Like you told me when we met, I'm a pawn. You want to get what you can out of me, but it only leaves me hanging. We need a better deal than this. Give me something I can work with." Jay hung up the phone, now disturbed, yet he still called Carmen back. She answered on the first ring as if she was waiting for his call.

"Where are you?" she blurted.

Though he was caught off guard by her tone, it was easy to match her anger and volume considering how his phone call ended with Grendel. "What do you mean? I'm out handling business." Jay left the deck, heading towards the salon. "You know what I do every day."

"And for one day you can't leave your businesses alone? Right now, I'm sitting at home with Patience and Veronica in front of me. Weeks ago I put reminders in your phone for all the meetings we have scheduled with them. You've missed three already. I even told you this morning that you needed to find pictures of your backyard so we can try and figure out the set-up. We needed those photos because we don't have time this month to fly to San Juan."

Jay raised both his brows as he suddenly remembered seeing the meeting reminder. He was in the middle of sending an email when it popped up on his phone. He had dismissed it without ever reading the details. He also remembered Carmen saying something about him bringing pictures. "Look, baby, I forgot. I'm out here working on stuff for the honeymoon and I got caught up. I'll make the next one."

"You say that every time we have this conversation. Do you even want to get married?"

Jay stopped in his tracks upon reaching the doorway of the salon. He met eyes with Gully who was still seated inside. "I can't believe you just asked me that."

"I'm asking because you're acting like you don't want this. I know you have a lot going on, but guess what? I do, too. Remember my conspiracy charge? Remember the night I got arrested right along with you because the police thought I was letting you house drugs in my company? Nah, you don't remember. You don't remember because it doesn't mean shit to you. Or what about the two fashion shows I'm finalizing? Or the fact I have six kids who need my attention. Oh, and I might as well add, I have another one on the way. If I can make time for this wedding, you can, too."

"Carm, I said I was sorry. I'll make the next one. I promise."

"No, you didn't say you were sorry," Carmen informed him. "That's the problem."

"Car—" he listened as she hung up. Unsure of what to think and feeling somewhat lost, he took the phone from his ear. A few curse words were mumbled under his breath as he debated his next move. He thought to head home yet he wasn't finished viewing the boat. On the other hand, Carmen already expected him not to show. If he left, her meeting with their wedding planners would be over by the time he arrived. It would work more to his benefit if he stayed. He could at least make progress on the honeymoon, since he hadn't contributed to the wedding.

"Were you supposed to be somewhere?"

Jay plopped down on the couch, now sitting at the opposite end of his cousin. "I'm always supposed to be somewhere. I keep forgetting about these fuckin' meetings. You gotta help me with this shit." Jay stared at his phone and immediately went to his calendar to see what other reminders were there. "I need you to put this in your phone so you can make sure I'm where I'm supposed to be. I can't lose Carmen over this. I refuse."

"Give me the dates and times."

Jay scrolled through his phone and gave Gully every single meeting reminder he could find. From what Carmen had stored, the next meeting was in about two weeks and the rest occurred more frequently as the wedding drew closer. "When that alert goes off, I don't care where we are. Drag my ass to that meeting."

Gully chuckled loudly as he saved the last meeting reminder. "I got you. You'll be fine. When we—" Gully stopped speaking when he heard the sound of vibration. When his cousin left the salon, he instantly became curious. From the mystery guy at King's wedding to the back to back private phone calls, he couldn't help but wonder what his cousin had gotten involved in.

"You better have something I can work with," Jay bellowed as he made his way on the deck. "I'm serious, Grendel. No games."

"I have something," Grendel declared.

His tone, now airy and relaxed, made Jay somewhat anxious. For Grendel to call him back that quickly, he obviously had found a way to meet his demands.

"I think we can agree that it's time for The White House to intervene. I've set you up a meeting with my uncle. His name is Andrew North. He's a part of the White House administration. He will hear all your concerns and make sure your demands are taken care of. You don't have to fly to DC. He'll come to you. Matter of fact, you should be getting an email from him soon."

It took less than a heartbeat for Jay's phone to alert him of an incoming email. When he pulled the phone from his ear, he saw the sender was indeed Andrew North. "I got the message. After I read it, I'll let him know if I'm willing to meet."

"Oh, you're going to want to," Grendel replied. "Hopefully, y'all can work out the details. As for us, our business is done. My uncle will take it from here. If we don't ever speak again, which I hope isn't the case, congratulations on your nuptials. I wish you and Carmen the best."

"We need it," Jay mumbled as he thought about their argument. He had a few more exchanges with Grendel before the call ended. When he returned to the salon, he found Gully still seated. "I need to get home. We can come back tomorrow."

"Whatever you want," Gully replied, rising to his feet.

They left the boat and made their way to the limo. Well aware there was a thick cloud of tension in his house, Jay made it a point to clear things up with Carmen before he did anything else. When he finally walked inside, he spotted her sitting alone in the home office. Several papers were sprawled out across the desk, some even on her laptop. "I know that face is because of me," he told her, stepping in the doorway. "I'm fucking up."

Carmen didn't look in his direction. She was still heated with him and while he was ready to make up, she had more to say. If the right words came to mind, she would leave him feeling like she did, neglected and overwhelmed.

"I know I keep saying the same things over and over again. Promises don't mean shit without actions. So, I'm gonna show you I'm serious about this wedding. I had Gully put all the meetings in his phone so he can help me remember. I just want you to know I'm not intentionally skipping out. I really am forgetting."

Jay studied her face as he waited for a response. Not much had changed of her expression, which made him walk further in the room. He even closed the door so they could have privacy. Instead of immediately trying to get her forgiveness, he pulled up a chair and picked up a few of the papers. There were mockups of various table settings for the reception as well as a blueprint of the set up for the ceremony. "I like this," he expressed, pointing at one of the pictures. "We can add a tent area in my backyard, but do you know what would be even better?" Jay turned the paper over and grabbed a pencil on the desk. He then drew a large rectangle on the blank side of the page.

Carmen rubbed her lips together as a small voice in her head told her to give him a break. He was obviously trying, which was better than what she'd received from him before. She looked at the paper he was holding, noticing the small circles he'd drawn inside the rectangle.

Once he realized she was looking, he continued his thought. "What if we used the pool in the backyard for the reception? We can put a long stretch of sturdy glass over the pool and have the reception on top. We're not inviting a lot of people, and I'm pretty sure we'll have enough room for a dance floor. I can even get some special lighting in there so when it gets dark, the pool can be lit in one of our wedding colors."

"We could also paint our names and wedding date at the bottom."

Finally hearing her voice, Jay set the pencil on the desk. "I'm serious about this wedding. Lately, I haven't been showing that side of me, but I promise, all that is going to change. I'm going to be more involved like I should've been in the beginning."

"You better," Carmen replied, rising from her chair. "I don't know what's going to happen if we have this conversation again." She picked up the rest of the papers, organizing the documents into a stack, which she set on top of her laptop. "Everything will be right here if you want to look at it. I'm gonna head upstairs. I'm done for the day."

Jay didn't pressure her into staying, but he did make sure to get a kiss before she left. To him, the kiss served as confirmation he was officially in her good graces. He still had a lot to prove, but at least he was off to a start. The only thing he had to do now was play catch up.

Once she left, he reached for the stack of papers. He reviewed each one until he was up to date. For Carmen to be the only person majorly contributing aside from the planners, she had put a major dent in the planning stage. There were still things which needed to be decided upon, which led Jay to grab a sheet of paper from the printer. He started jotting down ideas and by the time he was done, there was hardly any white space on either side of the page. He had come up with three different sample menus, a list of suggested performers and song selections, and even a floral design in case Carmen wanted a wedding arch. Certain it would give her the satisfaction she was looking for, he placed the paper at the top of the stack and headed upstairs.

13

Win Again
Spring

Throughout the last couple months, Carmen noticed a tremendous change in Jay's attitude. He was present at every meeting with their wedding planners, perfectly balancing their nuptials with not only the grand opening of Iceland, but also with his trial. That morning the verdict was said to be read and Carmen could already hear Jay preparing for it. She was in the bathroom, putting the finishing touches on her makeup when she heard a soft thud. When she peeked into their room, she saw him on his knees, his lips moving at a rapid pace. Not wanting to impose on his prayer, she went back to what she was doing.

Less than an hour before court, she would be lying if she said she wasn't nervous. She was cleared of her own charges weeks ago, but there was no guarantee he would have the same fate. The state of New York was determined to find a way to keep him locked away simply because he was a Santiago. They could never make charges stick against his father, one of the city's most notorious drug dealers, so it was like winning the Olympics whenever they were able to get Jay.

Regardless of the way she felt, Carmen knew she couldn't show it. If she showed even a hint of weakness, it could affect Jay's entire mood. He had already expressed a few thoughts to her, which made her think he doubted a positive outcome. She always managed to swerve his thinking, but it didn't mean the thoughts were completely gone.

"Did you want Cathy to come to the courthouse?"

Carmen closed her compact and slid it inside her makeup drawer. Recently, she hired her receptionist as her personal assistant and it was still taking some getting used to. She had forgotten Cathy was even downstairs until Jay mentioned her. "She can. I want you to have as much support as possible." She looked at Jay to catch his reaction. He still appeared uneasy, which told her his nerves were wearing on him. "You got this, baby. I don't know what you're worried about."

"We need to prepare both ways."

"Why?" Her face was now hard and stern. "What's the point of putting two million dollars in a wedding if we're expecting a guilty verdict? Don't bluff. You know you're going to win. If you didn't, you wouldn't be so involved in this wedding. Didn't you just do a fitting on your tux? I know you weren't doing it to waste time."

"Of course not, I…" Jay's voice trailed off as he heard Gully call his name from downstairs. About to tell him to hold on, Carmen encouraged him to do the opposite.

"Go tell Gully what you're thinking. I bet your cousin can talk some sense into you." She flashed him a smile, but as expected, it wasn't returned. Jay merely mumbled a few words under his breath as he left the room. However, Carmen's smile didn't last long. When Jay's footsteps faded from the room, she slammed the bathroom door closed. Her body slid against it, a silent scream pouring from her mouth as she clenched her pelvis in pain. *God, please, no, not right now, this can't be happening, no, God, no, not right now.*

"Traffic is backed up at the courthouse. Gully wants to leave now. Are you ready?"

Carmen reached for the doorknob and locked the door at the sound of Jay's voice. She couldn't let him know what was happening. He already felt like his back was against the wall and if she told him she was losing the baby, it would set off another trigger. As much as it hurt to do so, she shielded the agony in her voice. "Um, you might have to go ahead and leave. That breakfast casserole didn't agree with me."

"Damn, Carmen, you have to shit right now?"

The pain in her lower abdomen increased, resulting in her kicking hard at the wastebasket. The repetitive thumps prompted Jay to try and open the door. "Look, I'm going to be awhile," she yelled. "Have Gully drive you over. Roman can bring me once I'm done."

"Why did you lock the door? I can't talk to you while you shit?"

Carmen attempted to curse only for the word to come out as sort of a grunt. It only raised Jay's suspicions as he tried the knob again. *Just get the fuck outta here.*

"Okay, Peaches, you definitely aren't gonna let me up in there. Just text me once you're on your way. You know I can't do this without you."

Carmen's eyes narrowed as she watched a trail of blood trickle from her bare legs onto the floor. A wave of déjà vu flew over her as she envisioned herself in that same position almost a year ago. *God, help me. This can't be happening, not again.*

"Carmen," Jay called, not hearing a response. "Is it stuck in you?"

If she wasn't experiencing a miscarriage, Carmen knew she would've laughed. Since she wasn't in the mood to even smile, she gathered enough strength to address him. If anything, it would make him leave her alone. "I can't do this with you standing there. You're making me uncomfortable."

"Alright, alright, I'm out. Just make sure you send me that text."

"I will," Carmen screeched. She could feel the bleeding growing heavier and it made her wonder how far away he was. She got her answer when she heard the bedroom door close. The sound only provided temporary relief. The longer she sat there, the bigger the blood clots became. The mere sight of the ghastly material sent her heart rate skyrocketing until she heard a knock on the bathroom door.

"Carmen, it's Cathy, Jay told me to check on you."

"Is he still here?" Carmen shouted.

"He's getting in the limo. He said you were meeting him at the courthouse."

Carmen reached her arm up and unlocked the door. Halfway on her feet, the onset of a cramp made her fall to the floor. "I need you to get Roman. I'm having a miscarriage. I need to get to a hospital."

"Car-Car-Car," a round of stutters sounded out Cathy's mouth.

Carmen could hear her feet shifting across the carpet as if she didn't know what to do. "Get Roman," Carmen yelled. More stutters came out Cathy's mouth before Carmen heard her running out the room. Not too long after, someone pushed open the bathroom door, moving her out the way. When Roman came inside, he stood there wild-eyed, as he noticed the pool of blood. His shock didn't last long as he bent down and picked her up.

"Don't worry, Carm. I got you."

She heard most of what he said before everything including her vision began to fade. She fell in and out of consciousness several times, only catching bits and pieces of the conversation around her. By the time she was in the backseat of a limo, the words paparazzi and Puerto Rico had been tossed around. Unsure of what Roman and Cathy were discussing, she hoped they wouldn't tell Jay about the miscarriage until after his trial. The last thing he needed was any extra stress and if she could spare him, she would.

***

Jay stared at his watch as the time drew closer to the nine o'clock hour. Carmen still hadn't showed and according to Gully, neither she, Roman, or Cathy, were answering their phones. The lack of communication made him fidgety until his attorney, Gomez, reminded him of the media circus outside the courthouse. Various members of the press, fans, and paparazzi were present, creating somewhat of a raucous. The crowd of spectators backed up traffic, the scene worsening upon his arrival. Unsure of what it looked like now, Carmen could possibly be going through the same hell. That's if she showed up at all.

When the judge entered the courtroom, she still wasn't present. Neither was Gully although he had driven him to the courthouse. Jay rose to his feet, along with Gomez, trying to stay composed. Not once had Carmen missed one of his court appearances. However, out of all the days she could've played hooky, she did it on the day the verdict was set to be read. He wasn't necessarily angry, more nervous and worried than anything as he wondered what was keeping her.

"Back on record in the Santiago matter," the judge began after everyone was seated. "Mr. Santiago is present again with his counsel, Mr. Gomez, the People of New York represented by Mr. Leaks and Mrs. Johnson. The jury is not present. Good morning, counsel."

Jay listened as Gomez returned the greeting. When the judge resumed, he fought the urge to look behind him. It was pointless, anyway. He knew Carmen wasn't there. Her warm presence had faded as soon as he left her side. As a result, he was drained of much needed support. He barely listened to anything the judge said until the jury came in the courtroom.

"During the course of the reading of the verdicts," the judge stated, "it is mandatory that the audience remain calm."

Jay glanced to his right to look at Gomez. There weren't any stress lines on his lawyer's face. In fact, he appeared comfortable. Unlike himself, Jay wore his emotions on his sleeve. A series of negative thoughts hit him at full throttle as he visualized the future. The images spanned from Carmen mailing out postcards regarding the postponement of their wedding to King dressed in scrubs as he cut the umbilical cord of his firstborn child. He even saw himself, sitting in a cell as he taped a picture of Nyla, dressed in a cap and gown, on a cement wall. Examples of events he would miss, the images suddenly shifted to a more positive tone. He saw himself teaching Rakim to ride his first bike and even a glimpse of himself clapping proudly as Kristian and Akaila walked across the stage as college graduates.

Then, the images disappeared. His attention was swayed as the judge asked him to rise and face the jury. He did so, following the proper protocol though it felt as if his legs were going to give out. At the angle he stood, he was able to see Gully behind him as well as King and Malik. When he glanced towards the plaintiff's side, he wasn't surprised to see his fiancée's ex-husband sitting in the third row. Kane was called as a witness, but his testimony ended up aiding his defense. He acknowledged to the court that Blu attacked him purposely in retaliation for a failed business deal which led to the shootout at Blue Magic. In Gomez's opinion, Kane's testimony and the surveillance tape was enough evidence to win over the jury. If so, he was destined to find out.

"We, the jury, in the above-entitled action, find the Defendant, Jay Santiago, not guilty of the crime of murder," the clerk read. Gomez grabbed him unexpectedly, gripping him tighter after he was acquitted of each charge.

"Nyla won this case for you," Gomez whispered once they were seated. "That precious little girl won this. I knew the jury wouldn't be able to look past her crying in that limo."

Jay couldn't utter a response as he came to grips with the verdict. The news was still sinking in when he covered his face, his head dropping to his lap. Streams of hot tears ran down his face as he told himself it was over. Every charge against him was gone and when he walked out the courtroom, he would have a clean slate. Gomez rubbed his shoulder as he cried, yet the show of support and comfort didn't stop his tears. Neither did it calm his adrenaline or allow his heart palpitations to cease. None of it happened until the judge dismissed the court.

King was the first to reach him, grabbing him in his arms. A genuine moment, Jay held him for as long as he could until Gully broke them apart. "I need you to come with me," his cousin told him. "You gotta get outta here."

"He can't leave. He needs to talk to the press," Gomez interjected.

"The press can wait," Gully argued. "This story is going to be a hot topic for weeks."

"The press can't wait," Gomez shot back. "We just won. He has to say something."

Gully knew Gomez had no idea what was going on. While he didn't want to be the one to break the news, if he didn't say something, a dispute would ensue. "When you walk out that door, you're going to be hit with something major. Now, you can speak to the press, but it's like feeding you to vultures. You're gonna be forced to provide a statement for something you learned a minute ago." Gully stopped speaking to give everyone a chance to brace themselves. After a few seconds passed, he resumed. "I got Roman on the line right before the trial started. Shortly after we left the house, he rushed Carmen to the hospital. She lost the baby. When you walk out that door, the press is going to hit you with the news like a raging bull."

"Holy shit," Gomez mouthed. He abruptly fell in his seat. "This happened this morning?"

Gully didn't reply as he stared deep in his cousin's hazel eyes. Jay wasn't blinking, maintaining a hard gaze for what felt like minutes. "I didn't want to tell you like this. I just knew when you walked out the door, they were going to ask you about it. Roman and Cathy tried to keep it a secret. They think one of the nurses leaked the story."

Jay broke the gaze as he looked at King. They both were expecting babies that year, but now, he no longer was. His son's look of distraught didn't match a hundred times what he was feeling. The sudden high he was on was now brought to a place far deeper than a grave. "You can't have it all, eh?" He directed the question to Gully. "I win my fuckin' case, but I lose my child?"

"God works in mysterious ways. I can't tell you—" Gully was cut off as Jay's temper raged.

"You can't tell me shit. So what, I couldn't have both? It was either my freedom or my child? Was I supposed to choose?"

"It wasn't your choice to make."

Jay turned to King, hearing his voice. "I knew I shouldn't have left her. She was losing it right when I was leaving. She knew it, too. Why didn't she tell me?" His head shook repeatedly as he answered himself. "She knew I couldn't take it. I would've crumbled right then and there. I would've," an eerie cry of pain sounded out Jay's mouth as he envisioned Carmen bleeding on the bathroom floor. "I don't want this." He wept. "God can have it back. He can take my freedom. I don't need it. I want my child."

"The choice wasn't yours," Gully muttered. "It never was." He reached out for his cousin, but Jay moved away. Gomez signaled for him to leave him alone, which he did, allowing Jay space to grieve. No one spoke, not even the spectators in the back of the courtroom.

Jay wiped his face only to feel sweat beads on his forehead and stained tears on both sides of his face. He spoke softly unlike his usual deep drawl, addressing Gomez first. "The press is going to wait. Drum up a statement on my behalf. Say whatever you need to."

"I will," his lawyer replied. "If I had known about—" Jay silenced him as he stood on his feet. Now anxious to get to Carmen, he waited for no one as he quickly made his way towards the exit. They caught up to him in the hallway, shielding him from reporters and video cameras. There was an obvious lack of sympathy as people hurled questions about the loss at him. The monster within him wanted to unleash, but he couldn't. Gomez had fought too hard for him to catch another charge because a reporter was insensitive. Therefore, he maintained his composure.

They didn't escape the circus until they were behind the tinted windows of his limousine. Gully started a three-way call with Roman and Linx as they tried to figure out a course of action. They never came to a solid agreement until Jay proposed they spend a few weeks in San Juan. Far quieter than Brookstone, in terms of the press, the getaway could provide both relaxation and privacy. Jay felt it was the best idea at the time and expressed it to Carmen shortly after arriving at the hospital.

"My doctor told me I was taking on too much," Carmen replied, looking over what he said. "She said I needed to lighten my load. She wanted me to cancel my fashion shows. I told her no. She asked me how I was sleeping. I said barely. She even suggested I postpone the wedding. I told her I'm under several contracts."

Jay raised her hand to his mouth, resting it upon his lips. "You can't beat yourself up."

Carmen pulled her hand out his grasp. "I should've listened to her. Maybe if I had of, we wouldn't be in this situation." Carmen paused for a brief second. "I don't think I can do this again."

Jay took her hand back in his. He found her words disturbing as she told him she didn't want another baby. If stress caused her to miscarry, he knew they could lessen her workload. If necessary, he would take on extra duties around the house so she could go on bedrest. "I still want another baby. Do we need to wait? Yes. We should wait until after we're married. Maybe, if we do things the right way, the outcome will be different."

"You don't understand what I'm saying," Carmen stressed. "I don't want another baby." She pulled her hand out his grasp again. "My mind is made up."

Jay shook his head in disbelief. She was still operating off emotions, not giving herself a chance to heal from the loss or disappointment. "You can't make that decision right now. You can't make that decision for us. The wound is too fresh. You have to let this heal. We waited before; we'll have to wait again. Let's give it some time."

In Carmen's opinion, time wasn't what she needed. The decision was made hours ago when she was sitting in a pool of blood on her bathroom floor. Jay expected her to change her mind, but she wouldn't. Information he would learn whenever they revisited the conversation, she knew her decision could ultimately change the fate of their relationship. When it did, she only prayed she could stomach the outcome.

14

Lemonade

San Juan, Puerto Rico

Jay walked out of Carmen's hospital room, worse than when he first arrived. While there was grief over the loss of another child, he now grieved the thought of not having another one. Carmen's decision was understandable; however, she made the decision without thinking of him or their marriage. Although he didn't want to give up, Carmen wasn't willing to compromise. He asked her to try one more time, but Carmen wouldn't buy in. In fact, she told him she needed space. To make sure she got it, she asked him to go to San Juan to make sure the house was ready.

Jay respected her wishes and before she was even discharged, he returned home so he could pack his bags for Puerto Rico. Now at his San Juan estate, he stood outside the front door, eyes faced upward at the setting sun. *A beautiful sight for a depressing mood*, he thought. He shook his head at the visual before unlocking the front door. He then stepped inside, yelling Silvas' name. As usual, he dropped his duffle bags in the foyer. "Silvas," he yelled again when he didn't get a response.

He made his way towards the kitchen, already smelling his butler's cooking. The strong scent of peaches and bourbon tickled his nostrils as he drew closer to the room. Once there, he pushed open the swinging door to find two wine glasses on the kitchen's island. A bright red lipstick stain was on one of them, which sent a wave of déjà vu over him.

Dishes were in the sink and two wine glasses sat on the island. One of them even had a bright red lipstick stain. At the sight of it, Jay picked it up, carrying it in his hand as he retreated to the patio. It was there he found Silvas cleaning off the picnic table.

"So, you're bringing your dates to my house?" Jay joked, holding up the glass.

Silvas stumbled a bit, somewhat surprised that Jay was at home. Most of the time, he would tell him when he was coming. This visit, however, was a surprise. "No date, Mr. Santiago. I'm a little too old for that," he told him with a smile. "She was a visitor from America. She was sent by your psychiatrist, Dr. Stuart. Matter of fact, she came yesterday. I was too lazy to clean up so now I'm spending my afternoon straightening up the patio."

Like he had done earlier that year when he discovered Monifah had paid him a visit, Jay picked up the glass with the lipstick stain and headed for the patio. "Did this one belong to Monifah, too?" His butler was busy organizing a small stack of papers. "Or was this one actually a date? Let me find out you're getting some when I'm not here."

"You should tell me when you're coming."

"When did I ever have to do that?"

Silvas didn't answer the question and continued picking up the papers. He held the documents against his chest to keep the contents from being seen. "I shouldn't have said that," he mumbled. "It was wrong of me. I'm sorry. There is a lot going on."

"There is a lot going on," Jay repeated. He pulled out one of the patio chairs and sat down. "Since it's obvious you haven't been watching the news, I won my case." Jay listened as Silvas' excitement took over the conversation.

"See, I didn't even think about that. Of course, you won, that's why you're here. You came home to celebrate. Oh, and I made one of your favorite meals. Let me open a bottle of bubbly."

"That was number one. Two," Jay stressed, making the number with his fingers. "Carmen lost the baby this morning. The media is a bully right now. We can't stay in Brookstone or we'll be hounded everywhere we go. She and the kids are flying down in the morning. We're going to be staying here a while."

Jay watched as Silvas' face lost all signs of excitement. His butler now wore a frown as if he was seeing weeks of torture and aggravation ahead. "Come on, it won't be that bad. It's just us and the kids. Yeah, Gully and Roman will be popping in and out, but you ain't gotta act like that. You love Rakim and Nyla."

"If she knows you're here, she won't let up."

"Who?" Jay asked, looking around the patio. Silvas sat down, opposite of him, but didn't reply. Unsure of what he was thinking, Jay watched as Silvas reorganized the papers. "Are you talking about her?" Jay held up the wine glass, which resulted in Silvas giving him a head nod. "Who is it? You said it's not Monifah."

"No, Mr. Santiago, it wasn't. It was my daughter."

Jay's forehead naturally furrowed. "You never talked about your daughter. I knew you had one, but you were always sensitive about the topic. What do I have to do with her?"

"Y'all share the same last name."

Jay took a large swallow. Based off what his butler was saying, there was some sort of relation between them. Anxious to find out how, he looked around as if the woman was going to pop up. "I can't take much more. If you're saying what I think you're saying—"

"Her name is Eleise Santiago. She was born a few years after you in Brookstone, New York. She is your father's child. Now," Silvas paused when he saw Jay jump out his skin. "I have to tell you this now because Eleise is going to come back. Once she learns you're here, she's going to force this conversation on you. Please, don't say anything, just listen."

"How can I not say something when you're telling me my parents had another child? I spent my whole life thinking it was just me and I have a sister? So what, your wife couldn't have kids and they just gave her to you? You've been lying to me for forty-something years?"

"Yes, my wife couldn't have children, but that's not why I lied. I lied because she isn't your parents' child per se. She belongs to your father and Patricia Davenport."

Silvas' words were like a brick falling out of nowhere, crushing Jay's lungs. Everything his father taught him about family and trust was now a lie. Honesty and respect, the subjects of his late night talks with his father was now a bunch of bull. A devastating blow, Silvas continued to speak as if his world wasn't being sucked down a never-ending drain.

"Hector was hurt after Carmen's father left his cartel. He trusted Lotus more than anyone. He felt like his best friend turned his back on him. They became distant, but your father still watched every move Lotus made. He knew all about him changing his identity and becoming this Harold Davenport character. He never plotted against him until Patricia came to him for help. She was trying to make Flame a household name and at the time, all of Lotus' money was going into building up Davenport Realty. They had just gotten married, bought a house, and were trying to have a baby. Money was tight. Your father fed off his hurt and offered Patricia a deal. He would invest in Flame if she had sex with him."

"The apple doesn't fall far from the tree," Jay whispered. A fresh tear slid down his face as he saw a comparison in Carmen and her mother. Both of them had committed an act of betrayal to get money for Flame. Patricia cheated on Lotus while Carmen cheated on him with Carlos. They each had bedded their lover's best friend. Carmen's infidelity didn't result in a child, but her mother's had. Not only was he learning he had a sister, he was also learning his fiancée did, too.

"Patricia agreed to the deal," Silvas continued. "They had a one-night stand, Patricia got the money she needed, and that was it of the affair. A day or two later, your father came here and cried in my arms. It hurt him to his core. He didn't love Patricia. He didn't even like her. He had sinned against God, betrayed his marriage, his family, and his friend. He went against everything he believed in. It crushed him. He made it through until he found out Patricia was pregnant." Silvas paused, catching his breath.

"One day," Silvas went on, "Lotus showed up on his doorstep. They had a conversation where Lotus admitted his reservations about the baby. He claimed he hadn't touched her around the time she conceived. He said he was away on business a lot and didn't even need one hand to count the number of times they'd been intimate. Your father knew what he'd done, but of course, he didn't say anything. He made Lotus believe the baby was his, and at the end of the day, Carmen's father did. Eight months into the pregnancy, Patricia went into labor. Lotus was out of town, trying to secure a sale, and she went to the hospital without him knowing. After she gave birth, she called your father because she knew Eleise was his.

"Patricia immediately wanted her put up for adoption. Your father wasn't having it. At that time, he still didn't know for sure if she was his or not, but he wasn't going to let that happen. He claimed Eleise, made Patricia sign over her rights, and paid off the hospital staff. By the time Lotus got to town, they had a story together. He came to the hospital only to be told Patricia had given birth to a stillborn baby girl. He asked to see the child and was told the remains were already gone. Patricia told him she had the baby cremated. They even had a memorial. From what your father told me, Patricia went as far as letting Lotus buy a grave for fake ashes."

"Where did my father take Eleise?" Jay asked.

"He brought her here to Puerto Rico. My wife couldn't have kids. He gave her to us. By the time we got her, the DNA test was done. Eleise was definitely his. He paid us to raise her, but if you ask me, the money wasn't needed. Eleise is my daughter just as much as she is your father's. See, Jay, your father didn't make you and your mother travel back and forth between New York and San Juan because he loved Puerto Rico so much. He did it so he could remain in Eleise's life. He took care of her just like he took care of you. He loved her. She was his baby girl. Patricia, well, she hated her. She was a constant reminder of her sin. It wouldn't surprise me if Patricia has forgotten about her. I know for sure Lotus never found out about the baby and neither did your mother."

"Why is Eleise here?" Jay asked the question because he knew his sister wanted something. "She wants us to be one big happy family? That's not going to happen. Do you know how this would complicate things? I'm marrying my sister's sister."

Silvas' head dropped. "The situation is complicated. It's the reason I kept you two apart. I sent Eleise to Switzerland for college and it was the best news when she decided to stay after graduation. I knew I would miss her, but I couldn't risk you finding out about her. Now, that you know the truth, you can decide how you want to handle this business." Silvas didn't hesitate to slide over the papers. "Your father listed you and Eleise as his beneficiaries on several insurance policies and annuities. I kept these papers at my house to hide the secret from you and your mother. Your father took good care of Eleise, but she needs more money. She wants to open a business. The only monies left are the ones with both your names on it."

Jay grabbed the papers, quickly scanning each page. His mind worked like a calculator, adding up each figure and dividing it by two. "Silvas," Jay stressed each syllable as he realized the payday he and Eleise were looking at. "My father didn't invest his money in businesses. He invested his money in insurance. My mother had more money with my father dead than with him living. A lot of his drug money is right here. If I sign this, do you know what this means?"

Silvas nodded his head. "I know exactly what it means."

"I'm going to be a billionaire." Jay eyed every inch of the table until he spotted an ink pen. He grabbed it about to fill out the beneficiary forms until a disturbing vision appeared in his mind. He saw Carmen learning the truth of Eleise's identity and calling off the wedding. Then, he saw her ending their relationship using the words complicated and betrayal. "This could ruin us," Jay began, setting the pen on the table. "Do you know what this could do?" Jay looked at Silvas for a response. "What does it mean if I sign these papers? Is Eleise going to come around?"

"It's not all about the money. She wants a relationship with you. She feels its time. Y'all aren't getting any younger. I'm not getting any younger. She wants a family. She needs one. She's not married, she doesn't have any kids. All she has right now is me."

"Not like this," Jay argued. "She knows about me and Carmen, right?"

Silvas nodded his head. "She does. She's always kept up with you two. She knows all about y'all. Y'all just never knew about her."

"Then, she'll understand why she has to stay away." Jay rose from his seat and slid the papers towards Silvas. "I don't know what I'm gonna do about this."

Silvas parted his lips. "Jay, she needs y'all. I'm all she has and I'm not getting younger."

His butler's words were comprehended, but the matter was one Jay hadn't quite figured out. The payday was tempting, but if he signed the papers, Eleise might view it as an olive branch. The idea of her being in close proximity didn't sit well with him. He wasn't hurting for money although being a billionaire could open up a lot of doors. Still unsure of what he was going to do, Jay didn't respond to Silvas. He headed to his room, calling Carmen in the process. Judging from their last conversation, he almost thought she wouldn't answer. When she did, a slight breath escaped his lips.

"Thanks for checking in," she told him after picking up.

"You knew I was gonna call you."

"I actually wasn't sure," Carmen admitted. "I wasn't the nicest person to you a couple of hours ago. I told you to give me space and well, you did."

Jay stepped inside his bedroom somewhat unsure if he was supposed to be there. From what she said, it seemed as if she expected him to stay in Brookstone despite saying otherwise.

"You did what I told you to do," she continued. "It actually helped, I think. Being alone gave me a chance to really dissect everything. And, I can honestly say I was wrong. I shouldn't have made such a big decision. I," and she repeated part of what she said, "I shouldn't have made such a big decision for us. I need time to heal and process. I jumped so far left I didn't think about the impact. All you asked me to do is try. I should be able to at least compromise on that."

Jay sat at the edge of his bed, one hand holding the phone to his ear, the other wiping his face. "Marriage is about compromise," he said, a picture of Eleise now in his mind. "Be prepared."

"I should know more than you. I've been married before." Carmen listened as the phone fell silent. "I shouldn't have mentioned that. It's irrelevant. All that matters is our plan for the future. Tomorrow is a new day."

Jay remained quiet as thoughts of Eleise continued to circulate in his head. It was another secret to bear along with Casa de Sangre and the scandal in Africa. He felt somewhat weighed down. Nevertheless, he couldn't express his frustration out of fear of hurting her. He could only keep it bottled in. "We can get through anything," he said, quickly. "You believe that, right?"

"I do," Carmen agreed. "We're gonna get through this."

Jay parted his lips to respond until he heard Silvas coming up the steps. Certain he wanted to talk more about Eleise, Jay got ready to rush Carmen off the phone until she told him she needed to help Cathy. Perfect timing, he hung up the phone right as Silvas walked in his room. His butler dropped his duffle bags on the floor as if he'd been carrying a heavy load. "I was gonna get those."

"You know how I keep my foyer, Mr. Santiago. You're not twelve anymore." Silvas picked up one of the duffle bags and set it on Jay's bed. "Perhaps I needed the exercise. I don't do a lot of lifting around here." He picked up another duffle bag, which he also set on the bed. "I called Eleise after you left the patio. She has a flight to Switzerland tonight."

Jay felt a huge weight lift off his shoulders. With Eleise headed out the country, he had more time to figure things out. He strongly believed he would sign the beneficiary forms, but as far as a relationship with Eleise, the idea seemed foggy. "How can I sign these papers without her coming around here? How long will she be in Switzerland?"

"Eleise marches to her own drum. She's used to you not being here so she comes freely. She's gone now, but not for long."

"I figured that," Jay admitted. "I don't want to do anything to urge her to come. If only I could sign the papers and not deal with her." Jay rubbed his lips together as he thought the matter over. He didn't know Eleise like Silvas did so he couldn't say what she would or wouldn't do. All he could do was take a chance. Once his mind was made up, he told Silvas to set the papers in the parlor. Before he went to sleep, he would fill out everything and mail it off. He would give Eleise what she wanted. That way, before Carmen and the kids arrived, all paper trails of Eleise Santiago would be long gone.

15

Sorry

A month or so had passed since his conversation with Silvas in which he learned of his father's infidelity. He didn't speak of the issue to anyone, although he carried the burden. He wore the façade well and it helped that he and Carmen used most of their time to focus on Rakim and Nyla. Then, after a few weeks, they flew Patience and Veronica out to Puerto Rico to continue working on their wedding.

Currently, the ladies were sitting outside at a patio table, going over the set-up of the ceremony and reception. Present for most of the conversation, he stepped inside for a brief moment to make sure Rakim and Nyla weren't terrorizing Silvas. From what he found in the living room, they both were sleeping peacefully under Gully's watchful eye while Silvas worked on lunch. Roman and Linx were nowhere to be seen, but he figured they were somewhere around the estate.

When he ventured outside, he learned the conversation had changed. "I never found that design I did of my dress," Carmen was saying when Jay approached the table. "It's like it vanished into thin air." Carmen shook her head not knowing the design had been shredded by her ex. A while back, Kane had done a search of her office looking for anything that would implicate Jay and stumbled across the sketch. Upset over the fact she was planning a wedding when they weren't legally divorced, he destroyed the design. "So, I'm getting a French designer to help me create something. He's actually worked with Balmain."

"You didn't think about asking your mom?" The question was posed by Veronica.

Jay coughed at the mention of Patricia. The pure thought of her doing anything regarding their wedding was hysterical. The cough got him a side eye from Carmen who immediately made an excuse for her mother's lack of involvement.

"She's dealing with a lot right now," Carmen told them. "My father's passing is still hard on her. I don't think I'm gonna get her to do much of anything."

"She is coming to the wedding, though?"

Jay and Carmen met eyes at Veronica's question. Neither of them wanted to say the word no although that was the answer. Once again, Carmen tried to save face. "You know what," she began. "We have to take it day by day with her. Some days are good, some days are bad. We have to…" Carmen paused when Silvas approached the table. "We have to wait and see," she continued. "Right, Silvas?" She looked at him for a response although he didn't know what they were talking about.

"Right," Silvas replied as he poured each of them a glass of lemonade. "I hope I didn't keep y'all waiting long. I have a nice summer salad prepared as well as some of Mr. Santiago's favorite honey croissants. I won't spoil dessert. I want it to be a surprise."

Jay stood up once more as Silvas set a pitcher of lemonade on the table. "I'm gonna help you bring the food out. You don't need to be carrying all that by yourself."

"I kindly accept. I don't know where your muscle men are."

Jay chuckled at Silvas' description of his right-hands as he followed him inside. About to head in the kitchen, he stopped when he heard the doorbell. "Who made it past the gate?" He looked at Silvas questionably as if he was expecting a guest.

"I don't know. I'm not expecting anyone. You may want to check with Gully."

Jay did the opposite. Instead of going in the parlor where his cousin was, he went to the front door. He looked out the peephole only to see an attractive, middle-aged woman standing on the other side. A dead ringer for Paula Patton, he had to look twice to make sure it wasn't the actress. Once certain, he opened the door, which apparently caught her off guard. She jumped a bit when she saw him, taking a few steps backwards. "Can I help you?" he asked, remaining in the doorway.

"I didn't know you were here." Her voice was soft as if she was trying to be discrete. "Daddy didn't tell me you were here."

Jay's jaw clenched as he realized he was looking at Eleise Santiago. He studied her, examining every single feature. She had silky dark brown hair, which fell past her shoulders and a thin, but muscular frame. Her fair complexion matched his father's while she clearly had Patricia's eyes. When he noticed the resemblance, he joined her outside. He then closed the front door behind him. "You're not supposed to be here." Jay purposely walked in her body space until he had her standing a few feet from her car.

Well aware she was being kicked out, Eleise held up her hands in defense. "Can we at least talk?" Jay moved forward only to have Eleise place her hands on his chest to keep him at bay. "I didn't know you were here. I thought you were in Brookstone."

"So you thought it was okay to come?"

"I came to see my father," she admitted. "Is that a problem?"

Eleise sounded offended as if his words had struck a chord. She would soon learn her feelings were of no concern to him especially since Carmen was nearby. "Hector Santiago is your father," Jay corrected. "And he's dead. You can see Silvas all you want. You just can't see him here."

"Jay," Eleise began, saying his name rather matter-of-factly, "I know it's a delicate situation, but think about how I feel. I've been a secret all my life. I've lived in the shadows long enough. I can't do it anymore. I don't want to." Eleise loosened her grip eventually placing her arms at her side. "I know my timing is bad." Eleise began to talk a mile a minute about how she couldn't properly mourn when their father died or support him when his mother passed. Then, she turned on the waterworks.

By the time she was done speaking, her mascara had completely run and she had almost talked her lipstick off. "It's a messed up situation," he told her, "but it's also one that will hurt a lot of people. I wish we weren't in this predicament. You want a relationship with Carmen, I wanna marry her. You also want a relationship with me. I get it. It just can't happen right now."

"So when can we do it?" Eleise asked, wiping her face. "I know you signed the papers. Silvas told me you did. When are we all going to sit down? She needs…" Her voice fell silent as a new voice emerged. Jay closed his eyes as Carmen called his name from the front door.

"Are you talking to somebody? I thought you were gonna help Silvas."

Jay stared at Eleise as she looked to him for guidance. He then heard Carmen ask why he was in the driveway. Apparently, his size worked to his advantage as Eleise was hidden from her view. Then, the worst happened. Carmen walked towards them.

"Who are you talking to?"

Jay didn't move an inch although he answered her question. "One of Linx's exes came by." He met eyes with Eleise as he spoke, even balling up his fist so she would comply. He could feel Carmen breathing down his neck, which meant she had full view of Eleise.

Carmen was now beside him and she raised her eyebrow at the sight of the woman. Breathtakingly beautiful, she became suspicious although Jay said she was an ex of Linx's. "He isn't here," she told her. "In case you didn't know, he's married. He took the evening off to spend with his family." The woman looked at her dubiously as if she didn't know what to say. An uncomfortable situation, Carmen looked at Jay for help. He immediately took the hint.

"He's not here," Jay reiterated. "You can leave."

Eleise's face didn't lose its nervousness. In fact, it showed more when she took another step back. Then, she froze. "Can you at least tell Silvas I stopped by?"

"Silvas?" Carmen questioned. She looked at Jay for an explanation, but decided to go straight to the source. "You know him?"

"I'm sorry," Eleise muttered. "I need to go."

Carmen took a step forward as the woman got in her car. When the engine started, Carmen raised her hand to knock on the window. She believed there was more to the woman than being an ex of Linx's especially if she knew Silvas. Jay didn't let her, though. He grabbed her arm just as the woman backed out the driveway. He then reminded her of Patience and Veronica in the backyard. "So what was this about?" she asked. "I have to ask you since you wouldn't let me ask her."

"I don't know," Jay replied, heading inside. "I really don't."

Carmen looked at the front gate as the woman's car passed through. She wasn't quite sure she believed him, but the last thing she wanted to do was give the woman more of her energy. If she truly was Linx's ex, she was miniscule in Carmen's world. She barely knew Linx's wife so she definitely wasn't trying to befriend one of his exes. She decided to let the issue go and followed him inside. The woman wasn't fully wiped from her mind, but for now, she was a distant memory.

16

Forward
Summer
Brookstone, New York

Weeks since that day in San Juan, Linx's ex wasn't a thought in Carmen's mind. With less than six months until her wedding, her hands were too full to think of her. Not to mention, Jay never brought her up. She was easy to forget especially when Carmen was busy stressing herself over her wedding dress. Currently inside the design studio of Enzo Pierre, she stared at her reflection somewhat displeased with the gown. This was the third design they worked on. The dress was perfect on paper, but plain when produced. She wrinkled her face, an expression Tiara noticed. Her friend had accompanied her to give her input and it was definitely needed.

"What are you thinking?" Tiara asked.

"It's simple," Carmen expressed. "The sketch was amazing, the fabric was amazing, but it's simple. There aren't any stones, no beading, it's just a simple mermaid gown. I loved the design, but now that I've put it on, I'm not sold." She watched as Tiara moved closer for a better look.

"Look at the sheerness of this piece right here," Tiara stated, sliding her finger tips along Carmen's shoulder blade. "The way it falls from your right shoulder across your chest, it's what makes the dress pop."

Carmen bit her lip, unsure if she agreed. "Maybe, we could put some lace on it. Something to give it a little bit more oomph. Not on the sheer part or the train, but on the rest of the gown."

"Lace isn't going to go with this sheer piece," Tiara debated. "The two are going to clash. I think it looks great the way it is. We both know Jay has picked out some amazing earrings for you to wear. I also saw the bracelet he had custom designed for you. Once you put those pieces on with the dress, your hair is done, and your makeup is flawless, the dress will pop."

Tiara's words went in one ear and out the other. It didn't garner a response from Carmen partly because Enzo had returned to the room. He was holding Tiara's dress, which was still on a mannequin. He set it a few feet from them before coming to examine Carmen's gown.

"Uh oh, is it a no to this one, too?"

A loud sigh sounded out Carmen's mouth as once again she felt like she had wasted his time. "I'm just not sold." She changed her pose to see the dress in a different light. Still not pleased, she started to get upset.

"Everything is supposed to be bigger and better. I want Jay to look at me in a way he's never done before. This dress doesn't do it. I don't think the others did either." Carmen moved away from the mirror only to have a change of heart. The dress was materialistic and had nothing to do with the way Jay felt about her.

"Forget about it," she said, moving back towards the mirror. "I'm sticking with this. It just needs to be a little bit tighter around the bust and waist." Carmen looked at their reflections as Enzo pinned the problem areas. "Y'all have been so patient. What would I do without you?"

"I'll always be patient," Enzo stressed. "The more changes you want, the more I get paid."

Carmen laughed at his response until her phone rung from her purse. She asked Tiara to answer it when she recognized Jay's personal ringtone. "He knows I'm having my fitting. I wonder if something's going on." She listened as Tiara answered the phone, explaining she was still at Enzo's studio. Unsure of what Jay said on the other end, she watched as Tiara's mouth grew big. "What's going on?" Carmen moved away from Enzo although he was still pinning the waist area.

"Coco is in labor," Tiara replied. "Jay is on his way to the hospital."

"She's in labor right now? Like right in the middle of my fitting?"

"Babies do not abide by due dates, Carmen. They also don't care if you're in the middle of a fitting." Tiara chuckled at her friend's antics as she hung up the phone.

A loud grunt sounded out Carmen's mouth at the sudden change in plans. "We're going to have to reschedule. No telling how long Coco will be in labor."

"I know you don't want to miss it," Tiara voiced.

"I can't miss it," Carmen reiterated. She reached around towards the back of the dress and started to unzip it. "Enzo, I'll have Cathy contact you about another day I'm available. For right now, I need to get out of this thing." Carmen climbed out of the dress and changed clothes in a matter of minutes. Tiara decided to stay to complete her fitting so Carmen returned to her limo alone. Linx was waiting in the driver's seat with his phone glued to his ear. She could tell he was talking to Jay who was checking again to make sure she was on her way.

"Jay said traffic is backed up," Linx disclosed when she got inside, "but they should be at the hospital in the next ten minutes. We're not too far from there."

"Sounds good," Carmen mumbled as she buckled her seatbelt. "Hopefully this baby will hold off for a few hours. We need some time to get things together. I hope King had a bag ready. I wonder if he remembered the car seat."

"Are you about to freak out?" Linx peered over his shoulder. "There's no need for that. King and Coco have been preparing for this baby for a while. Besides, after that baby shower y'all gave her, she doesn't need anything. One more gift and she can't open the front door."

Carmen chuckled at his comments until his words reminded her of the mystery woman in San Juan. She never questioned him about her and with Jay not in the car, she could speak freely. "I forgot to mention this to you, but when we were in Puerto Rico, this woman came to the house. Jay said she was an ex of yours. She was light-skinned, had long, dark brown hair."

Linx looked at Carmen's reflection in the rearview mirror not quite sure who she was talking about. "Why would an ex of mine come to Jay's house? He doesn't know any of my exes. He only knows my wife. I don't know who that woman was."

"That answer doesn't surprise me," Carmen muttered. "Look, don't ask Jay about it. Just let it stay between me and you. I'll talk to Jay when the time is right."

"Whatever you want," Linx replied, continuing to drive.

Carmen shook her head at how Jay had fed her another lie. Not only that, the woman had gone along with it like she knew to play the role. Unsure of when she would question him, Carmen put the woman on the blackboard of her mind along with the other suspicious things he'd done.

Thankfully, she forgot about her when she reached the hospital. She rushed inside while Linx parked and reached the maternity floor to find Kristian and Akaila in the lobby. They told her Malachi was in Coco's hospital room with King so Carmen waited for Jay to arrive before she went inside. From what Kristian told her, Kane and Monifah were on their way as well. When Jay arrived, he appeared angry and she learned it was because his ten minute trip had turned into forty. A car accident had traffic backed up and he thought he was going to miss the birth.

"The baby isn't here yet," Carmen told him. "From the last update we got, this baby may not come until sometime in the morning. Coco isn't popping babies out quickly like I was."

Jay paced the floor trying to calm down. There was no need to be angry when he hadn't missed anything. "We're going to be here all night then." He was still pacing, but when Carmen grabbed his arm, he stopped.

"Do you want Gully to get Rakim and Nyla, or do you want them to stay at the house?"

"They can stay at home," Jay replied. "Your mom is supposed to be watching them."

"Well, do you want to head to the cafeteria? You look like you need a bite to eat."

"I'm good for right now," Jay answered. He sat beside her just as his phone rung. When he pulled it out his pocket, he wasn't shocked to see the name Andrew North. Grendel's uncle had been calling him for a while now. The only problem was that Mr. North called whenever he was dealing with something important regarding his wedding. Since he promised Carmen his full concentration, he missed every call. While he hadn't forgotten to return it, he barely had privacy. Even now, he couldn't have the conversation. His first grandchild was on the way and a conversation with the White House wasn't as important.

"Who is that?" Carmen asked as Jay ignored the call. "I don't know an Andrew North."

"He's a businessman," Jay explained. He shoved his phone in his pocket and quickly changed the topic. "Have you seen King?"

"Yeah, he came out the room for a bit. He's excited. Coco's parents are in there right now. The room isn't big so I didn't want us all in there with her. You know Kane is coming."

"I figured," Jay muttered. He gave Carmen a small smile to show he was comfortable having to deal with him for a few hours. "You know what," he said, changing his mind, "I do want something to eat. Why don't you come to the cafeteria with me?"

"I knew you were hungry," she joked. She picked up her purse and asked Kristian to text if there were any changes. After she agreed to do so, she and Jay headed to the café. Gully and Linx were already inside, stuffing their mouths so they joined them at their table. Delicious food and conversation helped the time to pass and before they knew it, the café was closing. Ten o'clock on the dot, Coco was still in labor, but the baby hadn't come.

It wasn't until two o'clock the next morning when Coco started to push. They crowded in the hallway outside her room until Carmen decided to sneak inside. She pulled Jay in the room with her and they watched the birth from a corner of the room. Not even two minutes later, the baby's head was out and then came arms, legs, and feet. Once again, there was an heir to the Santiago throne. Born Jayceon Santiago, Jr., the baby was nicknamed Prince from the womb. Born with a head full of beautiful, black, curly hair, he had dark brown eyes like his parents.

Full of emotion, Carmen watched as the obstetrician suctioned her grandson's mouth and nose before placing him on Coco's chest. Her daughter-in-law didn't look the least bit nervous despite her earlier reservations. From what Carmen saw, Coco had fallen in love. Certain Jay saw it as well, she looked behind her only to see him leaving the room. He was talking on his cell phone and she couldn't help but wonder what was more important than their first grandchild. Desperate to find out, she left the room, following behind him. He didn't go far, stepping inside a stairwell so she stood at the door to listen.

"I know I haven't been returning your calls," he was saying. "You texted me 911, though. What happened?" Carmen listened as a long stretch of silence appeared. "I can't help you right now. My first grandchild was just born. I'm getting married in a few months." More silence appeared. "This has to wait," Jay continued. "Right now, my family comes first. Until you or Grendel can tell me how you're going to protect us, I can't help you." Silence appeared again. "Okay, Mr. North, you don't understand what I'm saying. I'm washing my hands of this. I'm focusing on my family."

Carmen realized when Jay said the man's name that he was speaking to the man who called earlier. She was initially suspicious of the call and realized she had reason to be. She continued to listen until it sounded as if the call was coming to a close. Only then did she race back to Coco's room. By the time Jay returned, Prince was in her arms. She gloated over him, the baby taking her attention until she placed him in Jay's arms. As she watched him hold their grandchild, she couldn't help but ponder what he had going on. From the strange call on the balcony at Christmas to the woman in San Juan, she knew he was hiding something. He tried to wear a façade, but she saw right through it. Something was coming and she prayed he told her before it was too late.

17

Shanghai
December

Months since Prince's birth, Carmen's suspicions regarding Jay were officially on the backburner. With only days until their wedding, she was too swamped to pay attention to anything besides her nuptials. If anything did cross her mind, it was because it was brought to her attention. Such was the case when Kane called her right as she pulled up in front of their minister's house. She debated about answering since she was already late, but she figured she could spare at least two minutes. "You're lucky you caught me," she greeted. "What's going on?"

"I wanted to talk to you about Kristian."

A lough sigh erupted out Carmen's mouth because she knew why he was calling. Rumors about Kristian and Victor had been swirling around the house since last year. She assumed Kane knew about them since Kristian lived under his roof. "I didn't know if it was true or not because Kristian never came out and said it. I guess this wasn't some little crush like I thought."

"I want us all to sit down and talk," Kane responded. "This guy is in his twenties."

"I know," Carmen replied. "It bothers me, but for right now, they're just talking on the phone. She hasn't been to Georgia in a long time so at least we know they haven't been physical." Kane grunted on the phone, a clear sign the idea of Kristian being intimate didn't sit well with him. It bothered her, too, but Kristian was going to experiment whether they wanted her to or not.

"Can you come now?" Kane asked. "We're about to have dinner."

"I'm not having this conversation with Monifah," Carmen argued.

"You don't have to," Kane said, quickly. "She's still at work."

Carmen breathed a sigh of relief and told him she would be there in about twenty minutes. She braced herself for Jay's reaction once she told him she wouldn't be staying for their meeting. Thankfully, he was already inside with their minister, making small talk. She apologized for her tardiness before asking Jay if she could speak to him. Once he obliged, they stepped inside a small hallway while Bro. Harrison remained in the living room.

"What's going on?" was the first question out of Jay's mouth. "Gully told me you didn't want him to drive you. Is everything okay?"

"Nothing too big," she told him, giving him a quick kiss on the lips. "Something came up with Kristian and I need to go to Kane's house. I can't stay."

"Don't leave me with this man," Jay whispered. "Every time I look at him, I see every sin I've committed. Why would he let the devil in his house?"

"Shut up. You're not the devil." Carmen chuckled at Jay's words before giving him another kiss. "You'll be fine. Just pay him for officiating and leave. It should take you all of two minutes. Besides, once you're done, you can go to your bachelor party and relax. Matter of fact, once I leave Kane's, I'm heading to Blue Magic. Tiara and Cathy threw something together for me."

Carmen could tell her words were going in one ear and out the other. Jay still looked apprehensive like he didn't buy one word she said. "It'll be fine, I promise. Do what I said and go to your party." Jay narrowed his eyes, but she paid him no mind. Instead, she waved at Bro. Harrison, quickly telling him something had come up and that Jay would handle the particulars.

Fifteen minutes later, she was parked in front of Kane's condo. His Jeep was in the driveway, but Kristian's car was nowhere to be seen. She found it rather odd, but still rang the doorbell. Kane greeted her at the door and when she walked in the living room, she realized she didn't smell anything cooking. The only scent in the air was that of a cheap air freshener. "Where's the food? Where's Kristian?"

"Dang, Carm, take a seat. Let me get you a drink."

"A glass of Moscato," Carmen requested. She plopped down on the couch already reaching the conclusion that Kane had tricked her. There was obviously no dinner prepared and Kristian was probably at her house chilling with Akaila instead of in her room. "So what's going on?" she asked when he returned to the living room. He handed her a glass of wine, which she kindly took, but didn't drink. "I know you tricked me so get on with it. The quicker we do this, the quicker I can curse you and leave."

Kane sat opposite of her on a loveseat, both hands clasped together. He was starting to stall so she motioned for him to speak. Not a word was uttered, but he did stand and wander to his bookcase. He pulled out a stack of papers, which he brought to the couch with him. "I've been visiting Sanders a lot lately. He's getting used to his condition and trying to see how he can still work even from a wheelchair. It's no secret that the last case we were working on involved Jay."

Carmen set her glass of Moscato on the coffee table and stood on her feet. "This is some bullshit. So you called me over here to feed me some shit about Jay? Are you out your damn mind? Kane, we have moved on from this. I'm getting married whether you like it or not."

"I didn't go looking for this," Kane retorted. "But as a man who still cares about you, I at least have the decency to tell you your fiancé is stealing millions from you. He owns the house you live in."

Carmen's mouth was wide open at Kane's accusation. She never thought her ex would stoop so low. "Jay doesn't own my house. He never did. The house was owned by a private company. I worked with a real estate agent on the sale. I even met with one of the company's reps. I saw all the paperwork. In fact, I now own the house. I paid it off." Both hands were now firmly on her hips as Kane proceeded to lay the papers out on the coffee table.

"This," Kane stated, pointing at one set of documents, "lists the property under the ownership of Hector and Lady Santiago. Over here," he continued, "is the paperwork for where Jay had his parents' name removed and had the estate placed under his own company. Two signatures are on this document, one of them belongs to Jay, and the other belongs to his father's longtime financial advisor and lawyer." Kane paused for a brief second as Carmen eyed the documents. "I didn't go looking for this shit, Carm. Sanders found it and gave it to me. He doesn't have anything else to do with his time, but dig. He's paralyzed."

"Jay never owned my house. He only owns one house and that is the one in San Juan. The other house he owned he sold to pay King's bail from that jewelry store robbery years ago."

Kane shook his head in disbelief. "The house you live in is Casa de Sangre. It's the house Jay grew up in. Got damn, how did you not know this?" Kane pulled a sheet of paper from one of the stacks and showed her a photo of an estate identical to hers. The only difference was that the home lacked all the renovations that had been done on the property over the years.

As much as it pained her to cry in front of him, Carmen couldn't stop the tears from coming. She didn't want to admit he was right, but the proof was right there. The more she came to terms with it, the faster the tears came, caused by a range of emotions from betrayal to anger. She realized how easily her fiancé had swindled millions out of her. She also realized how naïve she had been. When she took the tour of the property, no one mentioned anything about it being owned by Hector Santiago or the site of a murder and suicide. She also didn't bother to ask. Even when she told Jay about the property, he didn't volunteer any information about owning the estate. Besides, he hadn't lived there in over thirty-something years.

"Let me take a closer look," she bawled. She picked up the papers, her hands somewhat shaking as she read the documents. Sure enough, the addresses matched, and she knew Jay's signature better than her own. "This doesn't make sense," Carmen cried. "His father was killed in our bedroom. His mother committed suicide in that house."

"I don't know why he did this," Kane replied. "You have to ask him. All I know is that I didn't want you walking in this marriage blind. You can do whatever you choose with this information. If you still want to marry him, go ahead, but you need to confront him."

Carmen sat down as she continued to read the papers. One hundred percent legit. Sanders had done a thorough search especially when she found a copy of her own offer to buy. The sight of it made her stack all the papers together. She set the documents in her lap not muttering a single word. Kane had placed a boulder on her chest and the weight of it was choking the life out of her. *Not a boulder*, she thought. *It's a bullet.* Carmen peered at Kane as she suddenly remembered the nightmare she had over a year ago.

From what she remembered, she and Jay were engrossed in an act of consummation only to be caught by Kane who shattered their moment with a single bullet. While she thought the dream had a literal meaning, she now saw otherwise. The bullet was only a material object to represent the papers she now held in her hands. Kane might not have been looking for a way to stop her marriage, but one stumbled in his lap and he used it. Sanders provided the bullet and he fired the gun.

"You don't have to rush home," Kane was now saying. "If you want to stay here and cool off, you're more than welcome. Monifah won't be home till eight."

Carmen shook her head. She had no intention of staying. She needed to get to Jay and she made sure Kane knew. "I'm taking all this," she told him as she walked to the door. "Every last bit."

"It's all yours."

His words didn't prompt a response as her anxiety worsened. When she left the house, she didn't even check to see if she closed the door behind her. Matter of fact, Carmen didn't even remember driving home. All she knew was that when she walked in her bedroom, Jay wasn't there. When she went downstairs to check the common areas, he wasn't there either. Only then did she venture outside to see his limo wasn't even in the driveway. For all she knew, he was probably at his bachelor party or still at Bro. Harrison's house.

In actuality, it was the latter. Jay was still sitting in Bro. Harrison's living room. The two hadn't even started talking so his visit was longer than he liked or expected. Bro. Harrison had taken a call moments before Carmen left and was still on the phone. Once the conversation ended, Jay made sure to speak first. "Carmen and I want to thank you for officiating. I'm here to pay the fee." Jay handed the check to Bro. Harrison, but he didn't take it. Instead, he motioned for him to keep it.

"I actually want to talk to you about why I can't officiate," the minister stated, plainly.

"I thought Carmen already discussed everything with you. She said we just needed to pay the fee and make sure your flight was taken care of."

When Bro. Harrison opened his Bible, Jay knew where the conversation was headed. He had spent many Sunday mornings listening to the man preach on the sanctity of marriage, the importance of being equally yoked, and how to maintain a healthy relationship with your partner. Well aware he hadn't fully devoted his life to God, he did expect the minister to stick to his word and marry them. "Mr. Santiago, you've been attending the church for some time now. You've heard years of sermons so I know you're aware of what the Bible says on marriage."

"The Bible says a lot on the topic. Which part are you referring to?"

Bro. Harrison closed his Bible, but Jay learned it was only because he didn't need it. He could quote the scripture from memory. "Whosoever putteth away his wife, and marrieth another, committeth adultery: and whosoever marrieth her that is put away from her husband committeth adultery." Bro. Harrison opened the Bible to that particular passage and handed the book to him.

"Luke 16:18," Jay replied, not looking at the page. "I know the scripture."

"When Carmen married Kane, she created a covenant that could only be broken in one of two ways: death and adultery. Now, I counseled her ex-husband when he first learned of Carmen's infidelity and I advised him to do one of two things. I told him he could reconcile and forgive his wife or he could forgive her and file for divorce. He chose to divorce her, but only after he committed adultery as well. That made them both ineligible according to The Word to remarry."

Jay sat up straight as he heard Bro. Harrison loud and clear. "I know what the Bible teaches. We all have sinned and we all have asked God for forgiveness."

"God does forgive, Jay. Still, according to the Word, a person who commits an act of adultery is ineligible for remarriage. You're aware of this, right?"

"Can we have a real conversation?" Jay waited until Bro. Harrison nodded before he spoke. "You know exactly who I am and what I've done. I've spent seventeen years in prison for things you've only seen in movies. Since the age of twenty-seven, no woman has loved me, but Carmen. No woman would. I've never had the desire for anyone but her."

"So you're marrying Carmen because you don't think you can get someone else?" Bro. Harrison spoke calmly as if he was trying to understand the gem of what Jay was saying. "You have been in a long term relationship with this woman. I do believe you love her and I know she loves you. Marrying her because you think no one else is out there is not a reason to get married."

"I know I can't get anyone else," Jay admitted. "But that's not why I'm marrying Carmen. I'm marrying her because she completes me. She counsels me through my mistakes and doesn't give up on me. She knows I want to be a better person. I'm showing her I can be."

"Jay," Bro. Harrison said, now sitting straight up as well. "This conversation is not about your character. This conversation is about what the Bible teaches. Aside from you and Carmen being unequally yoked, she cannot marry you."

"I have every intention to get baptized. I only want to do it on my time. As for us getting married, that's gonna happen whether you officiate or not."

Bro. Harrison swallowed. "That is what this conversation is about. I can't officiate. I wanted to hold this meeting so you and Carmen were both aware of why I cannot."

Jay stood on his feet and tore the check in two. Only a few days before they were set to walk down the aisle and Bro. Harrison decided at that moment to bail. His reasoning was understandable yet Jay believed he still should've carried out the ceremony. In his opinion, Bro. Harrison wouldn't be at fault if the marriage was against God's Word, only him and Carmen. If marrying Carmen was in fact wrong, Jay believed there was one loop hole to make it right. "There are only two ways out of a marriage, right? The wife is bound by the law as long as her husband liveth; but if her husband be dead, she is at liberty to be married to whom she will; only in the Lord." A direct quotation of 1 Corinthians 7:39, Jay watched as Bro. Harrison's eyes grew big. "So now I have to kill Kane."

A fear like he had never seen shone in Bro. Harrison's eyes. The minister was now sweating bullets. "Once Kane is dead, their covenant is broken. I make this vow today that I will never kill again after I take his life. I'll get baptized since you teach that baptism washes away sin." Jay watched as Bro. Harrison sat there speechless. Not one syllable sounded out the minister's mouth. Jay knew it was because he couldn't believe what he was hearing. "I have no ill will towards you. You're only doing what you feel is right. The sad part about it is that I am, too."

A look of fright was still on the minister's face and Jay could tell he was debating about what he should do and say. Since he didn't care for a reply, Jay excused himself. Once in the foyer, he finally heard Bro. Harrison speak.

"You can't manipulate scripture to justify wrongdoing."

"Who says I can't?" Jay shot back. "Ministers do it every day."

He waited for a response until he realized nothing more needed to be said. Bro. Harrison wouldn't be officiating and it was up to him and Carmen to find a replacement within the next forty-eight hours.

"Carmen has been trying to reach you," Linx announced once he was back in his limo. "I told her you were still talking to Bro. Harrison. You can try calling her back, but she said she was heading to Blue Magic."

"She's having her bridal shower there," Jay replied. "I need to talk to her, but I don't want to ruin her party. Bro. Harrison just bailed on us."

"Did he have a scheduling conflict?"

Jay shook his head, choosing to spare the details. Too upset to repeat the conversation, he asked Linx to take him home so he could get ready for his bachelor party. Even though Bro. Harrison had him troubled, he needed to release some much needed steam. Then, after a night of partying, he and Carmen could sit and discuss their options.

"You got a lot on your mind," Linx stated when he pulled in the driveway. "You hardly said anything the whole ride."

"It's like you said," Jay replied. "I have a lot on my mind." *Too much actually*, Jay thought as he got out the car. *I knew Carmen shouldn't have left me with that man. He wouldn't have said half the shit he did if she was there. It probably worked to his favor she left. He could speak freely about her marriage to Kane without her saying anything.* Still shaking his head over the conversation, Jay entered his bedroom and closed the door. He even locked it to ensure his privacy. From there, he stripped himself of his clothes, heading into the walk-in closet he shared with Carmen. As usual, everything was in its proper place until he threw his dirty clothes on the floor. To avoid an argument, he picked up his clothes and tossed the items in a hamper.

You can't manipulate scripture to justify wrongdoing. Jay rolled his eyes at the minister's words as he sifted through his clothes. *I'm not manipulating anything. Besides, I'm not gonna touch Kane. I was just fuckin' with you. I already have everything I want. I have Carmen. I have my freedom, and I have my kids. Killing him would be pointless.* He pulled out a dark denim jacket as well as matching jeans which he threw across the bed. He returned to the closet, pulled out a white t-shirt, which he eventually threw across the bed as well. He then opened up his jewelry case and picked out a stainless steel diamond watch. Once he had set it on the bed with the other items, he returned to the closet.

He had only taken one step in the doorway when he noticed Patricia. Not quite sure how she had gotten inside when he hadn't seen or heard her come in, he looked behind him at the locked door. He then looked at himself, a quick reminder he was standing in front of his fiancée's mother completely nude. "What are you doing in here?" he yelled. He grabbed a pair of Carmen's pants to cover his man parts. "How did you get in here?" Patricia didn't answer him, standing completely still, her eyes frozen on his. "What are you doing in here?" he repeated. When she didn't answer him, he walked further in the closet. She took a few steps back, which was when he noticed a section of the wall sticking out further than normal. He walked closer to it only to learn it was actually a door.

"You snuck in here?" Jay held the pants up against his groin as he brushed past Patricia. She wasn't speaking, probably fearful of being caught, as he noticed a secret passageway in the closet. "How did you know about..." Jay didn't bother to finish his thought. He didn't need to ask. Patricia was his father's mistress, if only for one night, and was also married to his father's best friend, Lotus. Anyone could've told her about the secret passage. *No one ever told me, though.* "Was this one of the secrets my father spilled when he fucked you?" Jay opened one of his drawers and pulled out a pair of boxers. He then grabbed a pair of sweatpants, which he slipped on.

Patricia's eyes grew big as she realized Jay was aware of her secret. She didn't speak on it, choosing to overlook the comment. "I married a man who knew the ins and outs of all types of real estate," she replied. "Lotus helped Hector with lots of properties."

"You shouldn't have even brought up Lotus," Jay spat. "Marriage doesn't mean shit to you. Family doesn't either. Your husband passed not even knowing you had another daughter. Tell me, Patricia, when was the last time you actually laid eyes on Eleise? Was it when you gave birth?"

"I don't know what you're talking about."

Jay chuckled at how Patricia was denying her own flesh and blood. "You know exactly what I'm talking about. You kept this secret for more than forty years. You would've gotten away with it, too. Your worst nightmare has now come to light. Do you know what I could do with this information?"

"Are you threatening me?"

Jay made sure to invade her body space. "When have I ever threatened you? Everything I ever said I would do to you, I've done."

"Your mother made that same promise."

A feeling of uneasiness settled over Jay as he took in Patricia's words. She was so close, he could snap her neck, but he didn't lay one finger on her. He only stared at her as he felt the memory of his mother's suicide creeping in his mind. *Only feet away from him was where he found his mother's body. A gun was beside her, a bullet was in her forehead, and a pool of blood was spreading across the floor underneath her. The only sound in the room was his screams. It was a noise he heard for hours until he finally was able to pull his body away from hers and dial 911.* A vivid memory, he saw that day as clear as he saw Patricia in front of him. So vivid, he could barely grasp how he didn't figure it out sooner. "You did it, didn't you?"

Patricia looked at him questionably almost as if she didn't quite understand what he was asking. Jay spoke sternly as rage started to build in his chest. "My mother found out about Eleise, didn't she? Lotus never found out, but my mother did. She threatened you. She told you she was going to tell Lotus the truth so you did what you had to do to protect your family."

"He was all I had."

The rage was now full blown. His hands wrapped around Patricia's neck as he tried to break it in two. She grabbed his arms to loosen his grip, but she was powerless against him. She struggled to breathe, something he wanted, but he also wanted her to suffer. It was the only reason he freed her. When he did, he punched her square in the nose. The blow sent her on the floor, prompting Jay to grab her legs and drag her from the closet to his bedroom. From there, he made her face his punching bag. She tried to block his fists, but it was to no avail. He punched her repeatedly, blood gushing from her mouth and nose as he beat her to a pulp. Just like he had cried out for his mother thirty or so years ago, he cried out for her again.

For years he tried to tell himself his mother wouldn't leave him. He told himself she didn't hurt herself although the evidence said otherwise. Now, as a grown man, he was learning his thoughts were indeed true. She didn't leave him, at least not at her own will. Patricia had stolen her from him. As a result, she had awakened a monster he kept buried deep within. The monster fed off pain and Patricia had given him his biggest meal. Even now, as she appeared unrecognizable, it wasn't enough. She had taken something from him that could never be replaced. For that, she needed to pay.

To make sure she did, Jay wandered over to the French doors, which led to the balcony. Nightfall covered the city while light fixtures lit up the estate. He couldn't think as his actions were controlled solely by his emotions. At that moment, all he could do was feel and what he felt was intense throbbing pain. Pain from losing both his mother and father, pain from spending seventeen years in a cold cell, pain from learning Carmen had married the man who imprisoned him, and pain from losing two children who never even opened their eyes. That pain led him back to his bedroom. That pain became externalized as he inflicted it on Patricia. By the time he was finished, she laid there motionless, her clothes rent, and her face bloody from where she had been bludgeoned.

Still, for Jay, it wasn't enough. Her condition was only miniscule. Therefore, he made his way back to the French doors, dragging her by the legs with him. Once he had her on the platform, he picked her up, holding her at waist level. No one was outside so he was certain no one heard the thud as he dropped her over the balcony. She landed behind a set of rosebushes right outside the home office. Now satisfied, he headed inside his bedroom, closing the doors behind him.

18

Trini Dem Girls

There was something different in his reflection as Jay scrubbed Patricia's blood and skin from underneath his nails. His eyes were bloodshot red, veins appeared out of nowhere on the sides of his neck, and he looked extremely manic. Not much changed once he was dressed, so he grabbed a pair of shades to cover his eyes. Not one to normally don sunglasses, Linx gave him a double glance when he walked in the foyer. Jay expected Linx to question him, but he didn't. Instead, he told him to get ready to have the time of his life.

"Malik and King got this place packed," Linx yelled once they were in front of Sapphire. "The whole city came out to turn up with cha."

Jay forced himself to smile as he stared at the long line of people waiting to get inside. The smile didn't disappear until he noticed the majority of people in line were male. "They let all the females in first?"

Linx laughed before telling Jay to go enjoy himself.

"You know something I don't know?"

"Something kind of like that," Linx responded. "I'll be inside in a few. I need to park."

Jay raised his eyebrow as the doors unlocked. Not quite sure what Linx was getting at, he stepped out the limo only to be greeted by the crowd. "Two more nights of being a single man," he joked as he entered. He grinned proudly in an attempt to conceal the madness which still roared inside. The façade paid off until he was approached by two half-naked women clad in royal blue bikinis. His eyes scanned the walls of his club as he took note of the various strippers in the building. Before he knew it, he was shouting for King.

Small stages covered the dance floor, stripper poles had been installed, and the club's bartenders had been replaced with topless women whose nipples were covered by small pasties in the shape of a blue diamond. "Hell fuckin' no," he spat. "Where is King?" he yelled when Nicholas approached him. "I told him, no strippers, keep it clean and classy. This party ain't for me. This is for y'all asses."

"Come on, Jay, loosen up. We wanted to send you off right. We all know you ain't had any fun in a long time. King just figured we would resort to the old days when Sapphire was a gentleman's club."

Still in manic mode, Jay jerked Nicholas up by his shirt collar. Seconds from causing bodily harm, he heard King in his ear as he tried to calm him.

"Come on, now, Pops. You ain't gotta do all that. Let's go to VIP and talk about this."

Jay looked to his right where King was standing. The sight of him brought him back to reality as he realized how he might have looked to the club's patrons. "I'm sorry," he murmured.

"It's cool," Nicholas replied. "You were caught off guard. I get it."

"See, we're all cool here," King bellowed. "Now we can all go and get a drink."

Jay nodded his head as he followed him to the VIP lounge. A long couch had been reserved for them, which was where he headed. His right-hands were already inside with the exception of Linx. Six open bottles were on a table in front of him so he grabbed the first bottle of Henny he saw and chugged most of the cognac down.

"You ain't going to make it if you keep going like that," Gully joked.

"I'm not trying to," Jay shot back. He chugged more of the cognac, resting himself on the couch as he studied his surroundings. Naked women were practically everywhere and so was the money. Not something he wanted to get used to. He told himself to enjoy the visual because it would never happen again.

"Go ahead and pick one," Roman quipped. "It's only a matter of time before they're headed this way."

Jay shook his head. The last thing he wanted was for someone to take pictures of him with a stripper. He had spent years trying to win Carmen's heart and the last thing he needed was her hearing about the bachelor party and calling the wedding off. They were too close to the altar for him to risk it for a lap dance.

"Oh, we already got one picked out for him," Nicholas added. "We know what he likes. He wants a chick as dark as midnight, ass like boom, boom, pow, and tits, which sit like two fuckin' melons. Trust me, Roman, we got the right one."

"I'll smack a bitch if she touches me," Jay shouted.

"You ain't smackin' anyone," King retorted. "It's a bachelor party. You don't think Tiara hired a stripper for my mom's party? Let's be for real, Pops." King was way off course, not aware his mother's bridal shower had turned into a full-blown counseling session. While the men were at Sapphire partying, Carmen and her friends were wiping tears and drinking wine as they discussed how Carmen should handle the news of Jay and Casa de Sangre.

Jay shook his head as he finished off the bottle of Henny. "Tiara knows better." He swallowed the last sip and set the bottle on the table. "I want all this shit out my club after this party's over. The last thing I need is people thinking they gonna get this every night."

"We're bringing in a lot of cash, Jay. You may wanna think about it," Nicholas voiced.

Jay shook his head once again, pushing his shades further on his face. As he did so, he spotted a curvaceous female making her way past VIP. She put him in the mindset of Carmen, possessing a rich chocolate skin tone amidst long locks of flowing jet black hair. Obviously a stripper, she was clad in a turquoise cage-styled panty and bikini bra, which barely covered her erect nipples. The sight of her tamed the beast inside him as her physical appearance became visually pleasurable.

"Do you want me to get her for you?"

Nicholas' question went ignored. The woman might have caught his attention, but he still wasn't going to risk marrying Carmen by allowing some woman to gyrate all over him. He was too close to the finish line to let it happen. Thankfully, Nicholas let the issue go. Perhaps it was because he was too busying getting his own lap dances to even think. Jay would admit it was entertaining, but only because the scene spoke directly to the Henny inside of him. If he was completely sober, he would've made his way out the club hours ago. Instead, he was stuck in one spot as the alcohol took over his senses. At times, he faded in and out of consciousness, barely aware of his surroundings.

"I think he ready for her," he heard Nicholas say.

In his head, Jay cursed him, but the words were never verbalized. His silence was taken as approval so it was of no surprise when he saw another stripper walk in VIP. The woman he had seen earlier, she was still dressed in the turquoise lingerie, but a diamond pendant was now draped around her neck. A piece he recognized from Iceland, he knew it had been given to her on purpose. He could see the pendant from a mile away since the club's blue lights were reflecting off the necklace's large stone.

"Take your time with him," Nicholas instructed.

Jay was well aware of what he meant, but couldn't respond as a result of the Henny. Not that it mattered, since Nicholas was leaving. Gully was still sitting inside, but when the woman grew closer to him, he got up as well. Roman and King followed behind him, leaving him alone with the stripper. He heard himself tell her not to touch him, but his words fell on deaf ears. The girl did the opposite, climbing on top of him, and straddling him. She then gyrated over him, allowing her large breasts to bounce up and down off his chest. The feel of it sparked only a hint of excitement until she switched positions minutes later. With her back now towards him, she lowered herself onto his lap, swaying her large derrière seductively over his groin.

A mixture of emotions overcame him as she enticed him. The sober voice in his head demanded for her to stop while the voice of Henny encouraged her to continue. The alcohol won the argument as evident by him reaching his sexual peak. For the first time in years, another woman other than Carmen had made him climax. He didn't think it was possible, but it had happened. The stripper knew what she had done because immediately afterwards, she gave him a small smile. If he returned it or not he didn't know. He only knew that when he looked down at himself, he suddenly became embarrassed at the imprint of his member. When she moved away from him, he stripped himself of his jacket and covered himself.

Minutes later, Gully returned to the lounge along with Linx and Malik. He didn't speak to any of them although a lot of smiles were tossed in his direction. He ignored their expressions, closing his eyes until he was woken up a couple of hours later. Gully was in front of him, the music now a faint sound in the background.

"Time to get you home," his cousin said in his ear. "The party is over."

Jay nodded his head and attempted to stand, but the alcohol hadn't quite worn off. Gully sensed his dilemma and grabbed his left arm, pulling it over his shoulder.

"You're all the way fucked up," Gully joked. "How am I going to explain this to Carmen?"

"Don't," Jay mumbled. "Have Linx drive around the city until I'm better." Whether or not Gully was going to respect his wishes, Jay didn't know. For now, Gully's only concern was getting him out the club. A few strippers were still in the building, but the one who gave him the lap dance was standing outside the club's entrance. A long jacket covered her frame, hiding the assets, which she used to pleasure him. "Give me a sec," Jay ordered, pulling away. He attempted to stand on his own, which he somewhat struggled to do. "Where are you headed?" he asked, now speaking to the dancer. "What's your name?"

The girl gave him another smile before telling him a name he didn't catch or was too drunk to remember. She told him she was waiting on an Uber so he offered to give her a ride. Gully quickly intervened, which resulted in him telling his cousin to back off. "It's just a ride. Chill out." Gully obviously didn't like his answer so he went back inside, saying he was getting Malik. Jay wasn't sure why his cousin was bothered. Linx was now in front of the club so he grabbed the girl's hand and escorted her to his limo. By the time Gully and Malik came outside, they were pulling off.

"Jay Santiago," the girl whispered, buckling her seatbelt. "So this is what it's like to be in your inner circle. Men at your beck and call, fly ass limos."

"Hard work will get you a lot of things."

"Did I work hard tonight?" She gave him another smile, an expression Jay now expected to see. "Is that why you wanted to take me home?"

"You worked a little too hard," Jay admitted. "It's been awhile since I've been with another woman." Somewhat embarrassed by his words, especially when he was almost a married man, Jay turned towards the window. Linx was now on the interstate and from the looks of things, he was leaving Brookstone. "You have me thinking about things."

"What kind of things?" the girl asked.

"Like maybe we should go and have a night cap." Jay watched as her smile disappeared. "Am I scaring you?"

"No, no," she said, quickly, "I just think you have things misconstrued. I don't entertain my clients outside of work. Your son paid me to dance for you. I did my job, but that was it."

Something told Jay to look in the rearview mirror and for a split second he met eyes with Linx. His right-hand was obviously listening and he prayed he kept the conversation to himself. The girl had turned him down, which he should have expected. He didn't know her from any other girl he passed on the street and she didn't know him. Like she had said, King had paid her to provide a service. "You're right," he told her, feeling somewhat ashamed. "I made a mistake."

"It's cool," she replied. When she turned towards Linx and gave him a Bronx address, he knew the night was coming to a close, and he was glad it was. Guilt chipped at him. *Was I really about to sleep with this woman? Was I about to risk my life with Carmen for a stripper?*

His thoughts embarrassed him and he didn't find relief until Linx pulled in front of the girl's apartment building. When she got out the car, the only word he could mumble was goodbye. He meant it, too. He never wanted to see her again. He remembered not wanting another woman to touch him, but now he had asked one for sex. So many questions were in his head, but at the end of the day, only one thing mattered. Carmen was The One and in less than forty-eight hours, the whole world would know.

19

Bed of Lies

Having slept some of the alcohol off by the time he returned home, Jay was left with a pounding headache. He was anxious to get inside and tend to it, yet something told him that wasn't going to happen. For one, Malik's car was in his driveway so he was obviously adamant about speaking with him. Jay knew the conversation was going to be centered on the stripper.

"I don't want any parts of this," Linx said when he put the car in park. "I'm sitting right here." He turned the car off and rested his head against the seat as if he was about to take a nap.

"I'll handle him," Jay replied. "Nothing happened so he can bitch all he wants."

Ready to deal with Malik, Jay stepped out the vehicle and headed towards the front door. Malik met him halfway already starting a verbal tirade.

"What was that shit you pulled at the club? You left with that girl?"

"Nothing happened," Jay told him, calmly. "We dropped her off in the Bronx."

"Did you forget you're getting married? The paparazzi were all over the place."

Jay rolled his eyes as he pulled his keys from his pocket. He grabbed his cell phone as well and was shocked to see the numerous times Gully and Malik had called him. His cousin had even sent him texts begging him not to have sex with the stripper. "Y'all are some fools," he said with a chuckle. "Nothing happened. Linx can vouch for me."

"It's not about that," Malik yelled. He pushed Jay hard causing him to stumble. Jay quickly caught his footing, which showed Malik he wasn't as drunk as he thought. "You're this close to marrying Carmen and you wanna go running after a stripper?"

Jay let out a nervous laugh because he knew he had come close. "She put something on me," he joked. "She rode me so good; she almost made me lose my got damn mind. I took her home thinking we could fuck." His chuckle disappeared as he remembered the severity of the situation. To make matters worse, he and Malik were no longer alone. Linx was still in the limo, but Carmen was walking towards him as if she was coming from the pool house. "You're still up?"

"Who are you talking to?" Malik turned around to see Carmen standing a few feet behind him. She was wearing a silk robe and her eyes were bloodshot red as if she'd been crying. "Shit," he mumbled under his breath. "What happened at your shower?"

"You can go now, Malik," she said, now standing directly in front of them.

"I think I better stay."

Carmen gave him a side eye. If he wanted to witness an argument she was going to let him. Besides, her anger wasn't directed at him. Her anger was directed at Jay, her fiancé who stole millions from her and according to his conversation with Malik, had also cheated on her with a stripper. "Do you remember when we said we were going to be truthful with each other?" Her eyes were now locked on Jay's. He knew he had been caught and it read in his facial expression. He looked like a sad puppy. "When we got back together, we promised each other we were going to do things right."

"Nothing happened," Jay replied, speaking of the stripper. "I promise."

"Something did happen," Carmen shot back. "You lied to me. You stole from me. For hours I've been trying to find out why. Did it bother you that I had more money than you?"

Jay wrinkled his face as he became confused about why Carmen was angry. He looked at Malik for help, but he wore a questionable expression as well. "I don't know what you're talking about. If this is about my inheritance, I was going to tell you on our honeymoon. I wanted to keep it a secret because I don't want the whole world to know I'm a billionaire."

"So then why did you need my money?" Carmen was now shouting, her voice loud enough to wake the kids. "I have the papers in the house. Kane told me everything. You sold me your house and then you moved in like you hadn't done a thing." Carmen's head shook in disbelief. "That's fuckin' grimy."

Jay couldn't speak as his heart once again started beating rapidly. At any second, it could beat right out his chest. Carmen had said a lot, but the only word that triggered him was Kane. He thought for certain her ex had moved on, but it was apparent he hadn't. He was still willing to do any and everything to keep them from being together. "I'm gonna kill him."

"You want to, don't you?" Carmen probed. "You do shit and then you want to make someone else pay. Not tonight, no, baby, you won't be doing that shit tonight. Tonight, I'm gonna kill you."

Malik stepped in between them when he heard the threat. "He's drunk right now, Carm. I don't even know if he understands what's going on."

"I understand," Jay yelled. "I heard everything she got damn said."

Malik raised his arms in defense now moving away from both of them. Carmen took advantage of it and moved closer to Jay. "It's always too good to be true," she said. "We get close to the finish line and then you fuck shit up. It's like you purposely damage everything you touch."

"I wasn't trying to do that," Jay explained. "I was mad. You had broken up with me and I was hurt. I saw an opportunity to get back at you and I took it."

"Oh, so this was some revenge shit?" Carmen shot back. "You were mad, because once again, you fucked up. Instead of dealing with the break up, you go and do some shady shit. You know what? It's not even about you selling me the house. It's about you withholding a secret. You don't think I would wanna know my bedroom is where your parents died?"

Instantly, Jay thought of Patricia. He didn't dare look at the rosebushes although something told him she was still lying there. "I'm sorry," he said, softly. "I made a mistake I can't undo. If you want, I'll give you every cent back."

"I don't need the money. That's chump change to you, anyway." Carmen moved away as if she was going to head inside. When she stopped in her tracks, Jay knew more was coming. She turned to him, her expression almost deadly. "Who is the bitch you slept with?"

"No one," Jay replied. "I didn't sleep with anybody."

"I'm gonna ask you one more time," Carmen yelled. "Who is the bitch you slept with?"

"Nobody," Jay snapped. "I just got a lap dance."

Carmen sucked her teeth not believing a word he was saying. She heard him clearly when he was speaking to Malik. "You think I'm stupid, don't you? I heard what you said."

"He didn't sleep with her," Linx interjected, no longer in the limo. "I was with him."

"Did I ask you?" Carmen walked towards Linx, which prompted Malik to grab her. "Stay in your fuckin' lane. You're the fuckin' help. Matter of fact, get off my property. Your shift is over."

Jay stepped in between the two. Her anger was his battle to fight and the situation would only worsen if everyone else got involved. "I'm telling you the truth." He paused for a bit to lower his tone. "I didn't touch that girl. I got a lap dance and that was it. It was a bad call. I apologize."

Carmen wasn't sure if she believed him. She broke free from Malik's hold and paced the driveway trying to gather her thoughts as the night continued to take an awful turn. "I don't know what to do," she cried. "I don't."

"Don't say that, Carm," Malik interrupted. "Y'all need to talk this out."

"Shut the fuck up," Carmen snapped. "Why are you even fuckin' here? You know what, don't answer that. You're here because you need to help him. All of y'all can help him pack."

"Don't do this." Jay knew he was hearing the onset of the inevitable. Carmen was about to call the wedding off. "Tell me what I need to do to make this right."

"Die," Carmen yelled. "I want you to die." She cried as she said the words because she knew it was the pain talking. She didn't have a filter when she was angry and her words could cut to the core. She only wanted Jay to feel the same pain she manifested inside. "I don't know if you slept with that girl. All I know is that hearing you say that made me question my worth. I've put years into loving you, gave you three children, but it means nothing if some little hoe can come, pop her booty and snatch you up. I shouldn't feel like I'm not good enough. I never should feel like that. The truth is, you're not good enough. You never were." Carmen wiped her face as the tears fell heavier than before. "The wedding is off."

Jay listened as expletives sounded out Linx and Malik's mouths. Neither of them should've been shocked if they were following the conversation. He knew Carmen was calling the wedding off. She wanted to hurt him. It was in Carmen's nature to make a person feel as much pain as she did. "I never meant to hurt you."

"But you did," Carmen yelled. "Kane should have never brought this information to me. As your fiancée, the woman who is supposed to be your wife in two days, you should've protected me. You didn't. You never will. You're still keeping secrets. I've watched you, those phone calls, that woman in San Juan, Andrew North, it's only more secrets." Carmen wiped her face, but it was pointless. The tears weren't going to stop. The tears never did. Jay was a man she had loved since she was twenty-one. Even when she gave up on him, she would always find the willingness to try again. However, this time, she couldn't. She no longer had any fight. Too weak to carry another burden, she finally gave up.

***

Linx drove away from the estate, but it was pointless. The distance didn't stop Jay's adrenaline or calm the ache in his heart. While the manic in him had been suppressed at his bachelor party, the events of the night had awoken the spirit once again. "Where's my shit?" he asked Linx as he searched the compartments for his pistols. His right-hand didn't answer, continuing to drive around the city. "Where's my shit?" he repeated. His question went ignored until he realized his right-hand wasn't answering on purpose. "I know you have it."

"You don't need it," Linx told him. "You'll only end up doing something you'll regret."

The response infuriated him more. If his life wasn't in Linx's hands, he would've sent him through the windshield. Since it was, the only thing he could do was continue to search. When he came up empty, he knew Linx had dumped his stuff somewhere. As long as they were driving around Brookstone, he wouldn't have access to anything. The closest he would get to a weapon is if Linx stopped at one of his businesses, took him back to Carmen's or even to Gully's. From the way Linx was driving, none of those places were on his agenda. Then again, as long as he was acting wild and senile, his right-hand would treat him as such. If he calmed down, he could at least get to his penthouse apartment. It was hard to do, but after two hours of sitting quietly in the backseat, he watched as Linx circled around to Carmen's estate.

"Stay in the car," Linx ordered. "I'm gonna grab some of your things."

"I wasn't going inside," Jay retorted. "I'm gonna get in my car and go to Gully's."

"You don't have your license."

"Then you can follow me."

Linx nodded his head and Jay listened as the doors unlocked. They left the car, but Linx headed for the front door while he went to the garage. Once there, he lifted the doors, the garage lights automatically turning on. At that very second, an expletive sounded out his mouth. From what he could see, each window of his Aventador had been busted out and all four tires were flat. To add to the damage, the car had been keyed. Nevertheless, the destruction didn't stop there. When he looked inside, it was far worse. The seat cushions had been ripped apart, the interior was cut up, and the inside smelled of gasoline. "This is some bullshit."

"She fucked this shit up."

Jay looked behind him to see Linx in the garage. "She wasn't coming from the pool house," he stated, thinking out loud. "She was doing this shit when we pulled up. She was about to light it on fire." Jay shook his head at how far Carmen had gone. "We gotta get this outta here. She put gasoline on the seats. If someone makes a wrong move, this bitch is up in flames."

"I'm on it," Linx replied. He pulled out his phone immediately calling a tow company he knew had dealings with Jay. "Someone just picked up."

As Linx tried to get someone to the house, Jay thought of Plan B. Nothing came to mind until he looked at the keys in his hand. On his key ring was the spare key to Carmen's Lexus. "Handle this shit," he told Linx as an idea came to mind. "I'll check in with you later." He didn't wait for a response as he headed to Carmen's car. He expected for Linx to stop him, but his right-hand didn't. He left the estate, anger, and fury leaving with him, as he drove to Kane's house.

20

Don't Hurt Yourself

Jay parked directly across the street from Kane's condo and stared at the two-level home. Due to the minimal amount of light, he used the flashlight on his phone to search Carmen's car. She rarely drove herself around town, but in the event she did, she always exercised her right to bear arms. It was the reason he expected to find guns stashed in the seats or consoles. Carmen didn't fail him when he discovered a small, silver pistol hidden underneath the passenger seat. He grabbed it, immediately checking it for bullets before he left the vehicle. Fully loaded, he checked his surroundings as he walked to Kane's front door.

Once on the porch, he saw how easy Kane made it for him to enter. While he didn't find a spare key under the welcome mat, he found one underneath a flower pot. Then, when he unlocked the front door, he learned the house alarm wasn't set. He walked inside, barely making a sound, and closed the door behind him. Wallflowers were plugged in several outlets throughout the home, giving off enough light for him to find the stairwell. The steps creaked as he climbed, but not enough to wake Kane or Monifah.

He had never been in Kane's condo so he came to a standstill when he reached the top of the steps. Every door was closed so he wasn't sure which room belonged to whom. Nevertheless, he took his chances and tried the knob of the door directly in front of him. It twisted easily in his hand and when he opened the door, he noticed the room was lit by a fragrance plug as well. Monifah and Kane were sleeping peacefully, each confined to their side of the bed. With no care for their slumber, Jay slammed their bedroom door shut.

Monifah was the first to wake, gripping the covers with one hand while shaking Kane with the other. She didn't stop until he put the gun at her temple. At that very second, Kane's eyes opened and when he reached for his own weapon, Jay turned the gun on him. "Uh unh, don't hurt yourself."

"What are you doing?" Monifah cried. "What is wrong with you?"

Jay ignored every word she said. "You told Carmen about the house?" He kept the gun pointed in Kane's direction as he moved closer to his side of the bed. "You're still pulling stunts." He tightened his grip on the trigger, which drew more sobs from Monifah. "Are you happy now? She called the wedding off."

"I didn't want her going in the marriage blind."

"You didn't want her going in the marriage at all," Jay shot back. He climbed on top of the bed, now hovering directly over Kane as he pressed the gun's barrel against his temple. He cocked it only for Monifah to grab his shoulder as she begged him not to do it. He pushed her off him, throwing her down on the bed. Kane used that small window of time to reach for his gun. Before he could grab it, Jay hit him square in the face with the pistol. Despite the large gash on the bridge of his nose, the blow didn't knock him out.

"I was going to tell her," he told Kane, now speaking at a normal volume. "I tried to tell her. I was—" Jay listened as a shrill scream sounded from outside the room. He looked around as if he could see where it was coming from, but the bedroom door was closed. "Who is that?" He looked at Kane for an explanation, but he didn't speak. Monifah didn't say a word either. As the screams continued, Jay recognized the voice. Kristian's shrieks of pain were beyond disturbing. Her trepidation was also a reminder of what he heard from his own daughter when they were getting attacked by Blu more than a year ago. Unbeknownst to him, Kristian's screams were a result of frequent night terrors she'd been having since her brutal rape at the hands of the same man.

Unsure of what to do, Jay looked at Kane, whose eyes were full of alarm. Jay could tell he wanted to tend to Kristian. He knew the feeling all too well. After he and Cesar had survived Blu's attack, all he wanted to do was hold Nyla in his arms. The memory alone was enough to make him lower the pistol. Perhaps, he now understood what Carmen tried to tell him.

You do shit and then you want to make someone else pay, she had said. Her words were truth. He would've stopped at nothing to make Kane pay instead of examining the man in the mirror. He could only imagine how it would be for Kristian to bury her father. She would never forgive him and neither would Carmen. "I'm sorry," he whispered. He climbed off the bed as Kristian's screams continued to fill the house. "I'm sorry," he repeated. He walked backwards out the room yet it was pointless. Monifah and Kane were frozen as ice. They remained that way even when he ran from the room. It wasn't until he was in Carmen's Lexus he saw a bedroom light come on. He was unsure of what was about to happen and didn't stick around to see. He simply threw the pistol in the backseat and sped off.

21

Sandcastles
Christmas Eve

It was going on almost four o'clock in the morning when Jay pulled in the driveway of Carmen's estate. He expected to see his limo parked outside the house, but it was gone. He pulled out his cell phone to see a series of missed calls and voicemails, mostly from his right-hands. They were all questioning his whereabouts. He didn't return any of their calls. He only wanted to leave the city as quickly as he could. For all he knew, Carmen had contacted their wedding planners and canceled the wedding. Once the sun came up, the estate would be a media circus as everyone wanted the story behind their breakup.

He knew he didn't want to be a part of a scandal and felt the best decision was to return to San Juan. The trip would give him the time and space he and Carmen needed until they were able to sort out their differences. He also could turn away the vendors who had already begun preparation for their wedding. The only downfall of the trip was that he would miss seeing his kids on Christmas. While he could FaceTime with them, it wouldn't be the same as having them in his presence. That was a dilemma he would have to figure out within the next twenty-four hours.

For now, he made his way to the pool house. He found Roman passed out on the couch still in his clothes from the night before. About to wake him, he changed his mind when he took note of his condition. Roman was too drunk to fly anywhere. He was better off buying a one way ticket to Puerto Rico than letting his right-hand get behind the wheel of an aircraft. Therefore, he left the pool house and went back to the driveway. When he did, he couldn't help but look at the rosebushes. Patricia was still laying there, her body motionless on the ground. The sight of her didn't prevent him from leaving the premises. With only one destination in mind, he backed out the driveway, taking the events of the night with him.

Meanwhile, Carmen watched him from her bedroom window. Not able to sleep, she heard a car in the driveway and got up to investigate. When she saw him, she didn't know what to think. She thought for a second he was going to come in the house, but he didn't. He went to the pool house, but only stayed inside for a minute or two. Then, he got in her Lexus and left. Unsure of what was going on, she thought to follow him, but, for what? She would only end up cursing him and demanding he return her car.

Nonetheless, he would've never taken her car if she hadn't destroyed his. She closed the curtains and moved away from the window. She headed in the bathroom, turning on the light once she entered. The first place she went was to the mirror to stare at her reflection. Her eyes were red from hours of crying and the bags under them were more visible than before. Disturbed by her image, she turned the light off and got back in bed. She tried to sleep, but every time she closed her eyes, she saw Jay in front of her, feeding her the same apologies, excuses, and threats as before.

Then, she saw his tears. She even felt his strong arms wrapping around her. She felt his breath on the back of her neck as he whispered words as sweet as honey. That was the side of him she loved. The side she treasured and needed. It was the side that led her to conceive a total of five times throughout their lengthy courtship. The downfall of that side was that it was only short-lived. In an instant, he could become a picture perfect portrait of a horrifying night. There also weren't any boundaries to his extremes. For that, she had to turn away.

Memories, both good and bad, lingered in Carmen's mind until she felt her eyes growing heavy. She fought against the sleep, but it was a bigger predator than she. Eventually her eyes closed and when she did finally wake, it was because someone was knocking on her door and her phone was ringing off the hook. She answered the door first and found Gully on the other side.

"You're not dressed," he said as if she should've been.

"I didn't have an easy night." Carmen yawned as she wondered what news Jay's cousin was there to bring. "What's going on?"

"We can't find Jay. He's not answering his phone."

Carmen didn't find the news shocking. She assumed Jay wanted some time alone like she did as they came to grips with the end of another failed engagement. "He was here earlier," she told him. "He has my car."

"Is it true you called off the wedding?"

The question hit a soft spot as she had to verbally confirm the decision. She didn't answer right off, taking a breath before telling him she did. Gully looked disappointed by her response. "We always hit a roadblock," she explained. "We get so close only for it not to work." Gully instantly tried to get her to rethink the decision. His advice was unwarranted so she was quick to interrupt him when she heard her phone ring. "It might be Patience or Veronica." She walked away from the door and picked up her phone to see Tiara calling. She also learned it was a little after seven.

"Finally, I got you on the phone," Tiara exclaimed when she picked up. Her friend didn't give her a chance to speak as she began to repeat everything Malik had told her about last night. Carmen hated to hear the details and after a minute, she stopped her.

"I can't relive this," she said, sitting on her bed. "It's bad enough I went through it."

"I guess I'll save you the details," Tiara replied. "I only called because I wanna know what it will take to make this wedding happen. Jay made a mistake, but what he did isn't as bad as some other things he's done. You've forgiven him before; I know you can do it again. Besides, Malik said Jay offered to give you your money back. If you want, I can get Malik to pick up the check."

Carmen's face scrunched up at her friend's words. "It's not about forgiveness. It's about trust. I can't marry a man I can't trust."

A loud sigh clouded the receiver. Tiara then started her rebuttal. "You know he's gonna earn your trust back. He always does. Y'all are like magnets. Y'all separate, but the second y'all get close, you're stuck together."

"Why are you pushing me to be with him?"

"Because I know you love him," Tiara answered. "I know your history with him. He messes up, y'all break up, and then months later, y'all are back smitten with each other."

This time it was Carmen's turn to sigh. "I appreciate the support and encouragement, but I made my decision. The wedding is off." Her words only brought more disappointment from Tiara's mouth. Her best friend tried to encourage her to give it more thought, but Carmen was fed up with listening. She quickly ended the call only to see Gully still in the doorway. This time, he was joined by Rakim and Nyla, both of them wrapped around his legs.

"What do you want us to do?" Gully asked. "We can't find Jay and we're supposed to be flying to San Juan in a few hours."

"The wedding is off," Carmen shouted. "Why don't y'all understand that? You don't need to go to San Juan." She turned away from him, disappointed she was getting out of character in front of her kids. "Y'all can do your own thang," she told him, getting up from the bed. She walked to the doorway, but didn't say anything to him. She simply picked up Rakim, placing him on her hip while Nyla went on the other. Gully seemed to catch the hint and when they climbed in bed, she heard the door close behind her.

The same thing happened at Jay's estate in San Juan; however, he was the one who closed his bedroom door. He came home empty-handed having left Carmen's car at the airport as he boarded the first flight out to San Juan. Certain Silvas was still asleep, he didn't wake him to let him know he was there. Instead, he got in bed and laid there until the sound of construction interrupted his sleep. When he got up to see what was going on, he heard his bedroom door open. He looked behind him to see Silvas, but he didn't speak. He turned his attention back to the window to see a group of men setting up a wedding arch.

"I thought y'all weren't coming until this afternoon. I haven't made breakfast."

"The wedding is off," Jay disclosed. "Kane told Carmen about the house." Not hearing a response, he turned away from the window. He looked at Silvas, noticing the look of shock and disappointment on his face. "I keep fucking up. I can't even blame her this time." He pointed at the window as he got back in bed. "You can tell 'em to stop. They're wasting their time."

"Has she issued a public statement?"

Jay shrugged his shoulders. "If she has, I haven't seen it."

"I won't turn anyone away until we hear something. She may change her mind."

Jay stared at Silvas. While his butler had faith, his was diminishing. "I saw the way she was. She's not changing her mind." He pulled the covers up to his chest as Silvas walked further in the room. "I should've told her about the house a long time ago." He paused for a bit as his agitation grew. "I got men outside putting together a freakin' arch that's not even going to be used. I got our names and wedding date painted in my damn pool, and for what? Now I gotta get somebody to paint over it."

Silvas stared out the window, watching as the men worked. He then looked at Jay to see tears falling from his eyes. "You need to call her. I know you said she called off the wedding, but she hasn't canceled anything. The caterers are going to be here in a couple of hours. When they show up, they'll be bringing a truck full of food with 'em." Jay turned over in the bed, giving him his back. Still not receptive to his suggestion, Silvas decided to give him some time to himself. He closed the curtains and left the room, closing the door behind him.

Hours passed and as more vendors came to the estate, Silvas returned to Jay's room. "The caterers arrived an hour ago. They're working on lunch and thawing meat for dinner. The wedding planners are asking for Carmen. They said she hasn't answered her phone all morning."

"Then tell them the wedding is off and send 'em home."

"Why don't you do that? This is your wedding."

"Get out my room, Silvas."

Mostly calm in times of distress, Silvas had reached his breaking point. He grabbed the covers, pulling the sheets off Jay in an attempt to get him out of bed. "Get up. I mean it. You're not doing this today. You need to go downstairs and send these people home. You signed the contracts, you wrote the checks. Go talk to 'em."

His butler's words didn't force Jay to move. When Silvas realized he wasn't going to cooperate, he threw the covers down and left the room. Once he was gone, Jay grabbed his phone only to see several missed calls and voicemails. None were from Carmen, which was the person he hoped had reached out. If she called him, he would know they still had a chance. Since she hadn't, they obviously were still over.

Although his butler didn't want to, Jay was certain Silvas had gone downstairs to announce the wedding was over. In actuality, Silvas had called Carmen. She was asleep in bed when her phone rung, waking both her and the kids. When she saw who it was, she answered because she knew Gully was worried about Jay. "Hello," she greeted.

"Carmen, this is Silvas. I need you to talk to Jay. Or you need to call these people because they're setting up all these decorations in the house; taking over my kitchen, but Jay said the wedding is off. Now, he's upstairs in bed, refusing to come down and talk to them."

"So he's in San Juan?" Carmen asked the question although she didn't really need clarification. Silvas had already confirmed Jay's whereabouts. "Just tell them the wedding is off and they'll be paid in full. It's a two million dollar loss, but we'll have to eat it."

Silvas cursed. "Why am I the one who has to make this announcement? Why didn't y'all take care of this before these people showed up? You called off the wedding, you deal with it."

The phone hung up loudly in her ear. The first time she ever heard Silvas raise his voice, she didn't quite know how to take it. Then, to make her feel even worse, Rakim asked a question she wasn't ready to answer. "Mommy, where's Daddy?" The solemnness in his voice brought tears to her eyes. While she could tell him his father was in Puerto Rico, he would want to know why. In addition, how was she going to explain why their father wasn't there on Christmas and why they didn't have any gifts? All of their presents had been shipped to San Juan because the plan was to spend the holiday there due to the wedding. There wasn't even a Christmas tree in the house. "Why are you crying? Where's Daddy?" Rakim touched her face, running his fingertips along her tears. The gesture made her cry even harder as she grabbed him in her arms.

"Everything is going to be okay," she told him. "Mommy and Daddy love you."

Whether or not it would be, Carmen didn't know.

Neither did Jay. Now, a few hours later, he had finally gotten out of bed. He learned Silvas hadn't told anyone the wedding was off when he looked out his bedroom window. Event planners were busy setting up the reception area while Patience and Veronica were running around his backyard barking orders. The sight of it all depressed him even more. Then, to add to the stress, he received a text from Malik stating he and his family was going to make the trip as scheduled. That only meant two things. No one had talked to Carmen and the noise level in his house was going to escalate. He didn't respond to the message, but he did lock his door so no one could bother him. He then got in bed as if he wasn't expecting anyone.

In the meantime, things were the exact opposite at Carmen's house. No longer in bed, she and the kids had both bathed and dressed. Now sitting in the kitchen, they were busy chowing down on nachos with Fiona and Cathy. No one spoke as there was a big elephant in the room. Carmen knew her maid and assistant wanted to know about the wedding, but were scared to ask. The only person who wasn't scared was Gully. When he walked in the kitchen, he went directly to her to let her know everyone's plans.

"Roman is going to fly us to San Juan. Everyone is going."

The words, *have fun*, sounded in Carmen's head, but weren't spoken out loud. The comeback would've been uncalled for especially since Gully only wanted to get to the bottom of things. Both she and Jay had put everyone in an uncomfortable position since no one had officially called off the wedding. From the way Silvas spoke, everything was moving right along. Carmen knew she was at fault for wasting everyone's time. While it hurt to admit it, she was actually somewhat on the fence about her decision. She got to that point when Rakim asked about his father. While she didn't want to go back to a situation that wasn't a hundred percent healthy, underneath the hurt, there was unconditional love. For that reason, she hadn't called her wedding planners to officially call it quits.

"What are you gonna do for Christmas?" Gully asked.

Carmen rubbed her lips together because the same question had crossed her mind. "I don't know," she answered. "I haven't made a decision." She looked over at Rakim and Nyla. They were still stuffing their faces not paying attention to the conversation. "So you say everyone is going?"

"Everyone," Gully replied. "It's too late not to go. Everyone has already shipped their gifts."

Carmen knew she had done the same so it almost seemed as if she was forced to go to Puerto Rico. In a way, Carmen felt as if she was being put on the spot. In a slick sort of way, Gully was asking if she was accompanying them to San Juan. Or in other words, he was asking if the wedding was back on. Carmen wasn't ready to make that decision, but Gully obviously wanted an answer. "When are y'all leaving?"

"Within the next two hours," he told her.

Carmen nodded her head. She looked at Fiona and Cathy, both of their eyes on hers. "I guess I need to figure it out, huh?" Carmen was well aware the clock was ticking. After sitting a few minutes in silence, she excused herself from the kitchen. She went upstairs for some private time, but when she passed her mother's room, she stopped. She hadn't seen her since yesterday morning and was shocked she had slept through her argument with Jay. She also hadn't heard her moving around the house. She knocked on her door, but it didn't generate a response. She then tried the knob and while the door was unlocked, it jammed when she tried to open it. "Mama, can you let me in?" When no response came, she tried to open the door again. "Mama, I need to talk to you."

When her mother didn't respond, Carmen looked through the crack in the door. From what she could see, there was a big lump in the bed. "Okay, you want to ignore me. I know you're not sleep. Can we just end this war between us? Please?"

Carmen didn't hear a single sound pour from the room. After a couple of seconds, she gave up. Their scorned relationship would never heal and it was time she accepted it. Besides, there were bigger things to handle than her mother's snotty attitude. She headed in her bedroom and then inside the bathroom where she knelt on the floor. For the first time in days, she prayed.

The same couldn't be said for Jay who was growing agitated at the noise outside his room. Even when the sky grew dark, people were still outside setting up for a ceremony that would never happen. Then, to make matters worse, Silvas was back at his door. "Mr. Santiago," his butler called. Jay didn't dare speak. Due to his lack of response, Silvas tried the knob. When he realized it was locked, he began knocking. "This has gone on long enough. Roman is here now. He's gonna knock the door down."

"Don't touch my door," Jay shouted. He sat up and looked at the floor. He could see a shadow so he knew someone was on the other side. "If he comes through the door, I have something waiting on him."

"We don't care about your threats. This has gone on long enough. We're coming in."

Jay pushed the covers off him. Despite the threat, he didn't dare grab a weapon for the sake of Silvas. Instead, he remained still until he heard the sound of someone pushing against his door. The noise sent him on his feet.

He hurried to the door and unlocked it. At that moment, Roman stopped pushing against it. Ready to address them both, he opened the door and instantly felt his knees become weak. Carmen stood in front of him, her hair swept gently in a bun, a light pink cocktail dress covering her frame. Her presence was a complete shock and it was nothing for him to fall on his knees. Automatically, he began apologizing. His words came out mumbles as he tried to explain himself until she stopped him.

"I hear you, baby," she whispered. She rubbed his neck, trying to soothe him as he bawled in her arms. "I hear you. We're gonna make this work. I promise. We're in this together."

22

Grand Piano
Christmas Day

Most of the house was still asleep when Jay left the estate. The only exception was Linx who was accompanying him since he was his driver for the day. Before the sun even rose, Jay woke him, telling him he had a meeting to attend. In true Linx fashion, his right-hand pressed him for details. All Jay gave him was the address where the meeting would take place. Then, when they were on their way, he called King, waking him out his sleep as well. The only difference was that he told him *they* had a meeting to attend. He gave him the address and advised him to wake Roman up since he knew his way around San Juan. King didn't seem pleased about the early rise, but his attitude changed once he reached the destination.

"This was the last place I thought you'd be."

Jay looked into the audience when he heard his son's voice. He was standing in a baptism pool at Iglesia de Cristo, a church he had frequented as a child with his mother. The church's minister was beside him while Linx stood in the first pew. "I think it was a shock to everyone," he admitted. He watched as Roman walked in the building, his right-hand taken aback as well. "Y'all can take a seat. Y'all are just my witnesses." Jay turned and faced the minister. "Everyone is here now. We can start."

"You're getting baptized?"

Once again, Jay faced his son. He thought it was clear what he was about to do, but King obviously couldn't believe his eyes. He knew it was a long time coming, but it was something he needed to do to clear his conscience. He wanted a clean slate before he married Carmen and he knew God was the only one to give it to him. "I am. I think it's time. It's something I'm ready for."

"I need to take a seat." King plopped down in one of the pews. Baptism was a big step on his father's part considering his horrendous past. "Do you think you can handle this?"

"Handle what?" Jay questioned. "You don't think I can live my life for God?" When King tried to explain what he meant, Jay cut him off. "It's time I lead by example. I've been through a lot, but God held my hand through it all. He gave me your mother back. He gave me my freedom. He gave me you. It's time I do His will." Not wanting anymore interruptions, Jay turned to the minister again. "I'm ready."

"Jay Santiago, do you believe that Jesus Christ is the Son of God?"

"Yes," Jay replied.

"With your confession that Jesus is the Christ, the Son of the living God, I baptize you in the name of the Father, the Son, and the Holy Spirit. Amen."

Jay closed his eyes as the minister placed his hand on his back, leading him into the watery grave of baptism. His entire body was immersed as he was washed free of every sin he committed. Left in the water was his days as a drug dealer, murderer, fornicator, thief, liar, and extortionist as he came up completely clean. A moment he wanted King to see, after changing into dry clothes and praying with the minister, he approached him. "I'm glad you came," he told him. "You understand I had to do this for me, right? I can't lead our family if I'm not following God."

"I understand why you did it," King told him. "You did the right thing. I'm proud of you."

"I always wanted you to say that." Jay hugged him only for their embrace to be interrupted by Roman who suggested they head back home. Apparently, Carmen had already called trying to figure out where everyone was. Although it was their wedding day, it was still Christmas, meaning there were a bunch of toddlers waiting to open their presents. No telling what Carmen was dealing with since it wasn't just their two in the house. "I guess we need to get moving." Jay looked behind him at the minister who appeared to be leaving as well. He thanked him for obliging his request and made his way to the church's exit.

✳✳✳

Carmen tightened her robe around her waist as she gazed outside the window. Less than five minutes before, Patience had entered her room, asking her to give a final approval on the décor. Jay supposedly had already done a walkthrough after the Christmas gifts were opened and it was now her turn. "I made sure Jay is in his room. Gully is gonna keep him there so he won't see you before the wedding," Patience had said. Carmen appreciated the thought, but they had already debunked the myth that morning. After what they survived, nothing could jinx their day.

Therefore, she didn't hesitate to leave the room and head downstairs. At the back of the stairwell, near the back door, two men were unfolding a white carpet aisle runner. She greeted them as she passed, heading outside. A total of twenty chairs had been placed on the yard and were divided into two rows. Space had been reserved between the rows for the aisle runner. As for the chairs, each one was draped in a jade green satin chair cover and accentuated with a saffron-colored sash, which had been tied in a bow. Carmen walked past the set-up to climb four short steps that led to the ceremony stage. She had already walked across the structure during rehearsal, but the wedding arch hadn't been completed.

Now, as she stood in front of its finished state, she took note of almost every detail. The arch was a little over eight feet tall, its steel frame covered in a white curtain. A jade green-colored sash was wrapped around each of the arch's pole to match the chair covers. To add even more flare, tucked inside each sash was an arrangement of satin roses. The material had been dyed the same color as the saffron sashes on the seats and the golden yellow popped amidst the jade green. Roses and greenery covered the very top of the arch while the backdrop was made of hanging crystals.

"How does everything look?"

Carmen looked over her shoulder to see Silvas at the bottom of the stage. "It looks even better than the samples." She shot him a smile before looking back at the arch. "This is probably the most action you've seen the backyard have in years." She moved away from the wedding arch and headed down the steps to meet him. While Silvas was Jay's butler, everyone would agree he was more of a father than a paid servant. He also was now their officiant. After learning of Bro. Harrison's refusal to carry out the ceremony, Carmen felt as if the wedding was doomed again. Upon learning of their dilemma, Silvas revealed he was an ordained minister, something she and Jay never knew. Before they could even ask, he had already offered to marry them.

"Everything looks beautiful," Silvas admired. "Why don't we walk over to the reception area?" He held out his arm, which Carmen kindly took. They walked slowly to the pool where a large, white frame tent covered the area. Five round tables were inside towards the far end of the pool while a rectangular-shaped table had been set at the head. Each table was draped in a jade green tablecloth while the chairs were covered in white seat covers and accentuated with a saffron-colored sash. For a personalized touch, each table donned a framed portrait. Some pictures consisted of only her and Jay while others were of them with their kids. The tables were already prepared for dining so Carmen didn't hesitate to run her fingertips along the edges of the fine china.

"I'm glad you changed your mind."

Carmen peered at Silvas hearing his words. She knew he always wanted her and Jay together, but the decision to go back to the relationship wasn't an easy one to make. "It all came down to love," she told him, "and forgiveness. I realized yesterday I still have some fight left."

"He's not an easy man to love. That I know. He's been through so much."

Carmen picked up one of the framed portraits. Enclosed was a picture of Jay with their youngest two. "He has. I'm sticking by his side, though. I'm here for the long haul." Carmen set the picture on the table. "Time is ticking. Do you want to escort me inside?"

Silvas held out his arm like he had done earlier. "I'd be delighted to do so."

Without hesitation, Carmen linked her arm with his. He walked her inside and from there he retreated to the kitchen while she went to find Patience and Veronica. The two were in the parlor meeting with the other event staff so she quickly gave them her stamp of approval. From there, she retired to her room where her glam team was waiting. They had spent most of the morning helping to prep the wedding party and now their full attention was on her. Once she sat in front of the vanity mirror, they immediately went to work.

Hours later, she was slipping into an ivory mermaid-styled gown, one of several designs she and Enzo had worked on. A totally different dress than the initial one she decided on, the gown was strapless with a sweetheart neckline. Enzo had even added a lace and crystal embroidery to give the dress more spice. She paired it with pear-shaped cluster diamond earrings, an early Christmas gift from Jay. Christian Louboutin was on her feet, the Follies Strass design, a shoe embellished with hand-placed crystals and a glittered heel. Now completely dressed, the last accessory she needed was her bouquet. Patience held the arrangement as she made her way to the stairwell while Veronica carried her train. Once they were at the bottom of the steps, Patience handed the bouquet over.

Carmen took her place in the procession behind the rest of the wedding party. Despite the small amount of people, the area quickly became noisy when everyone noticed she had come down. Then, as the musical prelude begun, the noise ceased. A soloist performed an acoustic piano version of John Legend's, "All of Me," as Jay and Silvas took the stage. The first time seeing her fiancé in his suit, the designer in her studied him from head to toe. He was dressed in a white tuxedo from the *King* collection with jade green serving as his accent color as evident by his bowtie and diamond cufflinks. Black Christian Louboutin Greggo Flats were on his feet, a shoe he picked out himself. Silvas, on the other hand, covered his suit with an all-white robe and golden stole.

The sight of them reminded Carmen there was no turning back. When the pianist transitioned to a cover of Leela James', "Fall for You," the processional began. Akaila and Malachi were up first, her daughter serving as her only bridesmaid while her son was one of two groomsmen. Akaila wore the same gown as her sister and Tiara, a one-shoulder saffron peplum dress, which accentuated their frames to a T. Kristian and Gully were next to walk, fulfilling the roles of maid of honor and groomsman. At that time, King took his place in line, her escort for the procession. The moment he neared her, their arms naturally intertwined.

"You know," he began, whispering in her ear. "You never asked me for it, but as the person giving you away, you should know you have my blessing."

Almost speechless, Carmen recognized her son's words to be more than a show of support. His statement was a representation of how much growth there had been in his relationship with Jay. She didn't hesitate to kiss her son's cheek. "I needed your blessing," she told him, "just as much as I needed you to walk me down the aisle." Carmen choked back her tears, a bigger task than she expected. When Tiara and Malik walked down the aisle as her matron of honor and Jay's best man, Carmen was certain she would lose it. Two of her closest friends, they witnessed her and Jay's journey from the very beginning. They had seen their trials, their tribulations, and their triumphs. Without them, Carmen knew she and Jay wouldn't have made it as far as they had.

The same went for Rakim and Nyla, a beautiful representation of the love she and Jay shared. Carmen watched as they each made their way down the aisle. Nyla went first, their only flower girl, while Rakim followed as their ring bearer.

"This is your moment," King said, interrupting her thoughts.

Indeed, it was. Carmen tightened her grip on her son's arm as she heard the voice of the male vocalist. He was singing the opening line of "When I First Saw You," a duet she fell in love with from the movie, *Dreamgirls*. She stepped on the white carpet, her eyes now on Jay's. Not having noticed it before, as she grew closer, she could see the tears building in his hazel eyes. She whispered *I love you*, the words only making him cry more. When she finally stood in front of him, his tears still hadn't ceased. Then, to make matters worse, he whispered *you're beautiful*, which made her shed her own.

"We are gathered here in the sight of God and these witnesses to unite Carmen Davenport and Jay Santiago in holy matrimony," Silvas begun. "As followers of Jesus Christ, they believe that God created marriage. In

Genesis it says, it is not good for man to be alone. I will make a helper suitable for him. So God took one of his ribs and closed up the flesh in its place. Then the rib that the Lord God took, He used to make woman and He brought her to the man. Carmen and Jay, you were made for each other. As you prepare to take these vows, give careful thought and prayer as you make them as you are making an exclusive commitment to each other."

Carmen held Jay's hands in hers, their eyes deadlocked. Silvas continued with his opening remarks before leading them in prayer. He concluded a minute or so later before announcing a reading of 1 Corinthians 13 by Roman. Jay's right-hand quoted the passage from memory, once in English, and again in Spanish. After he returned to his seat, Silvas spoke.

"Into this union, Carmen and Jay now come to be joined. If any of you can show just cause why they may not be lawfully wed, speak now, or forever hold your peace."

If any time Carmen expected to hear her mother's voice or Kane's, it was right then. Unbeknownst to her, her mother's remains were still behind the rosebushes. As for Kane, despite his altercation with Jay, he had no plans to stop her wedding. He didn't even come to San Juan. With everyone in attendance in support of their union, no one spoke. The silence prompted Silvas to continue with the ceremony.

"Marriage is about laughing in times of joy and comforting in times of sorrow. It's about sharing in dreams and building a home centered on Christ so you all are working for a common goal—heaven. I charge you to have agape love as this is the cornerstone of marriage." Silvas paused. "Now, it is my understanding you both have vows you have written. By tradition, we will begin with Jay as he shares with his bride words from the heart."

Overcome with emotion, Jay struggled to speak. When he realized his words were unclear, he took a deep breath. He started over, this time speaking clearly. "Carmen, you are the woman who I have loved a million times over. Before you asked me, I was yours. I saw you and there was nothing else that mattered in the room. I love what I know of you and have faith in the things I have yet to discover. We have been on many journeys together. We've seen the highest of highs and the lowest of lows, but this journey is different. On this journey, we're finally devoting ourselves to each other before Christ. I marry you today with no hesitation or doubt. My commitment to you is absolute. I promise to love you every day as Christ has called me to."

Jay's words made tears wail in her eyes again. She took a deep breath in an attempt to gather herself so she could say her vows. "Beloved," she began. "I take you as you are and offer myself in return. I also take you as the person who you are yet to be. I will celebrate your triumphs and mourn your losses as though they were my own. I will love you and always have faith in your love for me. I love you conditionally and without hesitation. I will care for you, stand beside you, and share with you all of life's hardships and joys."

Carmen meant every word she said. She promised to stand by her vows regardless of the upcoming challenges they might face. While there were some still on the table, she wasn't going to let it stop her from becoming his wife. They would simply work through it.

"Carmen," Silvas said, catching her attention. "Will you have this man to be your husband; to live together with him in the covenant of marriage?"

"I do," Carmen replied.

Silvas posed the same question to Jay, and when she heard him say, "I do," she felt a sense of completeness. That feeling of being whole was what she needed. She also needed to give Jay full commitment. By doing so, their bond was strengthened. Now officially Mrs. Jay Santiago, the rest of the evening was a whirlwind. While Carmen remembered exchanging rings, the official declaration as husband and wife and their first dance to, "A Couple of Forevers," it all flew by so fast. Time didn't slow down until the very next day. Currently engaged in an act of consummation, Carmen finally began to live in the moment.

Sneak Preview

The Diamond Tiara
Part VI of The Diamond Collection

1

Three days had passed since Carmen and Jay's nuptials. An elaborate affair that took place in San Juan, Puerto Rico, it was held on the most recognized holiday of the year—Christmas. Despite the holiday, the newlyweds set sail for St. Lucia shortly after the event. Their guests, however, remained at Jay's estate until the following morning. One of these guests, in particular, was Tiara Washington. Carmen's best friend and her matron of honor, she also holds the title as Vice President of Flame, a multi-million dollar fashion empire headed by Carmen.

Due to that title, Tiara was obligated to return home to Brookstone, New York, to handle business. Prior to heading to the office, she made a stop at her friend's estate. Her three-year-old daughter, Robin, was in tow, a child she shared with her husband and Jay's best friend, Malik. Typically her daughter would remain at home with a nanny, but she brought Robin to Carmen's house to play with Rakim and Nyla. It was time for her to be around kids her own age since it wouldn't be long before she started Pre-K.

As for the day, it felt no different than any other. The weather wasn't as perfect as it had been in San Juan, but it was still a regular New York winter. She arrived to Carmen's house to find Roman and Gully in the driveway. Both of them worked for Jay while Gully also had the pleasure of being Jay's cousin. From what they told her when she got out the car, they were waiting on contractors to arrive. The word KANE was currently emblazoned on the front gate and since Carmen no longer wore that last name, the gate was being reconstructed to read SANTIAGO. The contractors arrived a few minutes after her so she saw them after she left Robin inside with Carmen's maid, Fiona.

"Have a good day," she called to Roman and Gully. She waved to them as she opened her car door. After they waved back, she proceeded to get inside, but something told her to look at the house. Perhaps, she thought she could get another peek of Robin. Whatever the reason, nothing prepped her for what she saw. Yards away from where she stood, she noticed a body lying at the base of the house. The lifeless figure was hidden by large rosebushes so it didn't surprise her she hadn't noticed it earlier. In fact, for a few brief seconds, she blinked her eyes to make sure she saw right. However, she didn't need confirmation. A dead body was in front of her whether she wanted to believe it or not.

Quite naturally, she screamed at the top of her lungs. The noise signaled Roman and Gully as well as the contractors who were getting out of their trucks. They ran towards her, grabbing her, yelling in her ear, but the image in front of her overshadowed it all. It took a few minutes for her to calm down and when she did, she pointed at the body since her words were indistinct. It was enough to get Roman to walk in the direction of the rosebushes. When he neared the corpse, she turned away, burying her head in Gully's shoulder. Certain Roman was about to move the body; she listened as Gully told him not to. The estate was now the site of a murder, which meant no one could touch anything. They were all suspects meaning they were each guilty until proven innocent.

***

Saint Lucia

Carmen picked up a piece of melon from the fruit bowl and slid it in between Jay's lips. He chewed the fruit rather quickly, which prompted her to grab another. Before she could slide it in his mouth, his lips became centered on hers. His tongue fought its way inside her mouth while his hands gripped her inner thighs. Once again, they devoured each other.

That was the scene the night before. At the current moment, things were quite different. The fruit bowl was broken, the glass pieces scattered across the kitchen floor. The walls and countertops were now decorated in a wide array of colors from where the fruit had been thrown about the area. Also, no one was in the kitchen. In fact, they weren't even near each other. Jay was upstairs in the master bedroom while Carmen was in the living room, lying on the couch. Her hair was unruly, there were scratches on her hands, and her knuckles were bruised.

Jay didn't look any better. He was bruised as well and there was even a small cut on his foot from stepping on the broken glass. Everything about his current condition was his fault. If Carmen hadn't gathered herself when she did, he knew the damage could've been far worse. Thankfully, she tired herself out and he was able to separate from her. Not once had he fought back and he didn't intend to. He also never got the chance to fully explain his actions. However, a chance was given when her phone suddenly rung from the bedside dresser. When he peered at it, he saw Tiara's name on the screen. Although it hurt to move, he grabbed the phone and slowly made his way down the steps.

Carmen heard him coming and it wasn't long before he appeared in front of her. Her phone was no longer ringing so she didn't bother to take it from him. She also didn't want any interaction with him. He caught the hint and set her phone beside her on the couch. When he did, Tiara called again. At the sight of her best friend's name, Carmen wiped the tears from her face because she knew why her best friend was calling. Less than eight hours ago, she listened to her husband of less than four days confess to killing her mother.

Carmen didn't know why nor had she asked any questions. She simply turned into a madwoman—screaming, yelling, punching, kicking, and unleashing all the anger she could. She was the reason the kitchen looked like a war zone. In a short amount of time, they had gone from making love to a one-sided brawl. Now, it was obvious that the news of her mother's death had reached Tiara. Her friend was still calling yet Carmen didn't answer. Eventually, Jay answered the phone.

"I can't understand you," he said, loudly, to Tiara. "Put Gully on the phone. You said he was there. Put him on the phone."

Carmen couldn't bear to listen when Jay was the reason her mother was dead. She grabbed the phone from him and when she put it to her ear she heard nothing, but commotion. "Tiara?" she called. "Tiara, are you there?"

"She's gone," she heard Tiara say. "I'm so sorry, Carm. She's gone. Her face, her face is…It's so bad. I'm so sorry." A cry of pain sounded on the phone followed by heavy breathing. "When they pulled her out, bugs were all over her, she had bite marks. She was behind the bushes. They left her at your house. Your mom…" Tiara cried. "She's dead."

Time froze. Or at least that's what Carmen perceived. It was like everything had stopped. Then, slowly, time started again. She already knew her mother was dead. She just didn't expect for Tiara to be the one to find her or for her mother to be found on her property. She thought Jay had dumped her mother's body somewhere else like he did his other victims.

"The police are still here. They only told us a few things," Tiara continued. "I called you as soon as I could. I had just dropped Robin off when I saw her. They asked me so many questions, Carm. I don't know who did this. She was right there. If it wasn't for her hair and if I didn't know her shape, I wouldn't have known it was her. She looked like Emmett Till."

"Where are my kids?" Carmen suddenly became frantic as she thought of Rakim and Nyla. The last thing she wanted was for them to be staring out the window as their grandmother's body was photographed and examined. "They don't need to be there. Get them out of there." Carmen headed for the front door, but it was pointless. She was too far to even get to them. "I don't want them seeing this."

"Fiona has them. She's keeping them occupied," Tiara disclosed. "I'm so sorry, Carm. I know this is your honeymoon. I didn't want to call you. I wanted to wait until you got back, but I couldn't."

"I know," Carmen muttered. "You had no choice."

Carmen swallowed as Tiara began to give her condolences. It hurt to hear it because it was only confirmation that both of her parents were gone. At the thought, a cry of agony sounded out her mouth. Tiara was still on the line crying as well until Carmen dropped her phone on the floor. The sound signaled Jay who came in the hallway. All it took was one glance in his direction before Carmen charged at him. When she did, he caught her, binding her arms so she couldn't strike him. He held her in place until she tired herself out and was only crying in his arms.

As he comforted her, he decided to tell her the truth. He needed her to understand and he hoped to get some compassion. "She killed my mother," he said in her ear. Carmen's sobs slowly turned to sniffles as she digested his words. "My mom was going to tell your father about her affair. Your mother cheated on your dad with my father," Jay continued. "She did it to get money for Flame. My mother found out about it and was gonna tell. That's why your mother murdered her. I didn't know about the affair until months before the wedding. Silvas told me. I didn't mention it to your mom until the night of my bachelor party. I caught her in our room. I confronted her about it and she confessed. That was when I did what I did."

Jay's words made Carmen nauseous. She covered her mouth to keep from vomiting as the news settled in. It was too much. All of it was too much. She couldn't hear anymore. Her mother was dead, her mother cheated on her father, and her mother killed his mother to keep the secret from coming to light. *This isn't real,* Carmen thought. *It can't be. This is only a nightmare. I'm gonna wake up and things will be fine. I know it will. This is just one bad dream. I just need to wake up.*

Carmen never woke up. As time passed, the nightmare only proved to be reality. More calls were made to her since she was her mother's next of kin. People gave their condolences; reporters requested an interview; police tried to contact her. She tried to make as many decisions as she could, but there was only so much she could do from St. Lucia. She was left with no choice, but to secure a flight back home. Still, she couldn't leave until she and Jay had a solid plan on how they were going to handle things. While she was angry and hurt over what he'd done, she felt those same emotions towards her mother. It was the reason she had every intention of helping Jay cover up the crime. His involvement in the murder would remain a secret unless evidence proved otherwise. At that point, he was on his own. As for their relationship, she considered him her husband only on paper.

www.ingramcontent.com/pod-product-compliance
Lightning Source LLC
Chambersburg PA
CBHW051843170626
46807CB00003B/1324

9780988800458